Redemption of the Broken

Katrina Case

© 2024

All rights reserved.

No portion of this book may be reproduced without written permission from the publisher or author, except as permitted by U.S. copyright law.

Chapter One: The Road South
November 1933

    The wind howled through the narrow streets of the small northern town, biting at Nathan Grant's skin as he pulled his coat tighter around his body. It wasn't cold enough for snow yet, but the bitter northern air still clung to his bones. His boots crunched on the frozen dirt road as he walked past rows of shuttered shops and dilapidated houses, their windows boarded up like the hollowed eyes of men who had seen too much.

    This town—like so many others—was a stop on his way to nowhere. He didn't even bother remembering its name. What did it matter? Each town looked the same to him now, worn down by the weight of the Great Depression, and the people inside it were no different from the ones he'd left behind in the last place. Towns like these were full of folks just trying to survive, clinging to what little they had left, and Nathan was passing through.

    The sky above was gray, heavy with the threat of snow, and the distant sound of a train whistle echoed across the valley. Nathan had considered hopping a train south, but he didn't have the stomach for it. Too many drifters and stories of men meeting an untimely end under the wheels. No, it was better to stick to the roads, no matter how long and cold they might be.

His mind wandered back to his parents, as it often did when he was alone. His father had been a carpenter, a good man with strong hands and a quiet way about him. Nathan had learned everything he knew about working with his hands from his father. But the elder Grant had passed away years ago—pneumonia had taken him, just like it would later take Elizabeth. As for his mother, she had followed her husband to the grave not long after, her heart broken by his passing. Nathan had been a grown man by then, already working in the city, starting to drift away from the faith that had once been a part of his life.

That was before the crash. Before he lost everything.

He shook the memories away, focusing instead on the road ahead. It was a familiar routine now—letting the past come close enough to remind him of what he had lost but never letting it linger long enough to consume him.

A small general store stood at the corner of the street, its sign swaying slightly in the wind. The dim glow of a single lantern flickered inside, casting long shadows on the frost-covered ground. Nathan hesitated. His stomach growled, and his throat burned from thirst, but his pockets were empty, save for a few coins he had earned working odd jobs at the last place.

The door creaked open with a groan, and the warmth inside hit him immediately. The smell of wood smoke and baked bread filled the air, making his hunger sharper. An old man stood behind the counter, his gray hair thinning and his face as lined as the cracked walls of the store. He glanced up at Nathan without much interest.

"Help you?" the old man asked, his voice gruff.

Nathan kept his gaze low, pulling the few coins from his pocket and setting them on the counter. "Just some bread and water," he muttered.

The old man stared at the coins for a moment before nodding and disappearing into the back. Nathan leaned against the counter, letting the heat from the stove thaw his frozen hands. His thoughts drifted to Leslie and Elizabeth—his wife and daughter. Leslie's laughter echoed in his mind, soft and sweet, and he could almost see her tucking Elizabeth into bed, the little girl's golden curls framing her face as she smiled up at her mother. But the memory shifted too quickly, turning to the day he had received the news of their deaths, and a cold dread replaced the warmth that had filled him moments before.

The old man returned with a loaf of bread wrapped in brown paper and a tin cup of water. "That'll do ya," he said, setting the items on the counter. "Not much else I can give you for what you got."

Nathan nodded, handing over the coins. "It's enough." The old man's eyes lingered on him a moment longer. "You passing through, I reckon?"

"Yeah," Nathan replied, picking up the bread. "Heading south."

"South, huh?" The old man shook his head. "Ain't much down there neither, not anymore. Folks think the cold's better up here, but the way I see it, hard times follow you wherever you go."

Nathan didn't respond. He knew the truth of that better than most. He took a sip from the tin cup, feeling the cool water slide down his throat. It wasn't much, but it would keep him going for a bit longer.

"You got a name?" the old man asked, his voice cutting through the silence. Nathan hesitated for a second.

"Grant," he finally said. "Nathan Grant."

"Well, Mr. Grant," the old man said with a half-smile, "you watch yourself on those southern roads. They're just as unforgiving as the northern ones."

"I'll keep that in mind," Nathan replied, tucking the bread into his coat pocket.

With a nod of thanks, he stepped out into the cold again, the door creaking shut behind him. He started walking south, his eyes set on the horizon. The town behind him, the unknown place with its worn-down shops and empty streets, would soon be just another stop on his endless journey.

But something felt different as he walked. The farther south he traveled, the more the landscape began to change. The bitter cold started to ease, replaced by a milder wind hinting at Tennessee's warmth. He had been heading south for weeks, but he felt something stirring inside him for the first time—something more than just the need to keep moving.

Millbrook. That was the name of the town he had heard about from a few travelers. It wasn't much, just another small place in a long line of small places, but something about it lingered in his mind. Maybe it was just the fatigue of the journey, or maybe it was something else. Either way, he found himself walking toward it.

The wind began to lose its bite as Nathan drifted farther south, the harsh chill of the north slowly fading into something milder, though the cold still clung to the early November air. The landscape changed around him as well. The endless fields of barren farmland gave way to rolling hills dotted with leafless trees, their branches scratching against the overcast sky.

In the distance, he could see the faint outline of mountains rising up like silent sentinels, watching over the land. Nathan's steps were slow and deliberate, each one measured against the exhaustion that had been building inside him for months. He had walked hundreds of miles through countless towns and still felt no closer to whatever he was searching for. Redemption? Forgiveness? He wasn't sure. Maybe he was just trying to outrun his past.

He adjusted the strap of the small bag slung over his shoulder, his fingers brushing against the loaf of bread tucked into his coat. It wasn't much, but it would keep him going for a while longer. The road stretched ahead of him, winding through the hills, and Nathan followed it without thinking. Just keep moving, he told himself. One foot in front of the other. Don't stop.

As the sun dipped lower in the sky, casting long shadows across the road, Nathan noticed a change in the air. It smelled different—cleaner, fresher. And there, on the horizon, he saw the faint outline of a town.

Millbrook.

He had heard about it from a few travelers back in the last town, though they hadn't said much. It was just another small town in the south, clinging to life in the middle of the Depression. But something about the name had stuck with him. Maybe it was how it sounded—solid, like a place that had weathered more than its fair share of storms. Or maybe it was just the fact that he was tired. Tired of drifting. Tired of the weight pressing down on him every day.

As Nathan approached the outskirts of Millbrook, he slowed his pace, taking in the sight of the town. It was small, no more than a few dozen buildings scattered along the main road, their wooden facades weathered and worn by time and the elements. Smoke curled lazily from the chimneys of a few houses, and the faint sound of laughter echoed from somewhere nearby, though the streets were mostly quiet.

He paused for a moment, his eyes scanning the town. It looked like any other place he'd passed through, but something tugged at him—a feeling he couldn't quite shake. There was a stillness here, a quiet resilience in how the buildings stood against the sky. He wasn't sure if it was hope or just another illusion, but he felt the urge to stop for the first time in a long while. To rest.

Nathan continued down the road, his boots kicking up dust as he walked toward the center of town. The street was lined with a few small businesses—a grocery store, a blacksmith shop, and a diner with a faded sign hanging above the door. A group of children ran by, their laughter filling the air as they chased each other down the road. Nathan watched them for a moment, a faint smile tugging at the corner of his mouth before he turned his attention back to the road.

He passed by the blacksmith shop, the sound of hammering ringing out as Earl Wilson, the town's blacksmith, worked at his forge. Earl glanced up as Nathan walked by, wiping the sweat from his brow with the back of his hand. "Need something fixed?" Earl asked, his voice gruff but not unfriendly.

Nathan shook his head. "Just passing through," he replied.

Earl nodded, his eyes narrowing slightly as he studied Nathan. "Well, if you need work, I could always use an extra pair of hands around here. Not much pay, but it's honest work."

Nathan hesitated for a moment, considering the offer. Work meant staying, and he wasn't ready for that yet.

"I'll keep it in mind," he said finally before continuing down the road. As he reached the town center, Nathan spotted the small wooden church standing at the end of the street, its steeple rising against the sky like a solitary beacon. The building looked old, its paint peeling and its windows clouded with dust, but something about it drew Nathan in. Maybe it was the quiet strength the church seemed to exude, or maybe it was just that he hadn't stepped inside a church in years.

He stood there for a moment, staring at the building, his mind churning with memories of his past. His mother had been a devout woman, her faith unshakable even in the darkest of times. She had dragged Nathan to church every Sunday, her voice rising in hymns of praise, her hands clasped in prayer. But after she died, after Leslie and Elizabeth, faith had slipped away from him like water through his fingers. Now, he wasn't sure if he even believed in redemption anymore.

The sound of footsteps behind him pulled Nathan from his thoughts, and he turned to see Reverend James Matthews walking toward him, a warm smile on his face. The reverend was a tall man, his hair streaked with gray, and his eyes were kind, though they held a depth of understanding that only came from years of watching people struggle through life's hardships.

"Afternoon," Reverend James said, extending his hand. "I don't believe I've seen you around here before. New in town?"

Nathan shook the reverend's hand, though he kept his gaze low. "Just passing through," he said, the exact words he had used with Earl. "Well, you're welcome to stay a while if you need to," the reverend replied, his tone gentle but firm. "We don't get many visitors in Millbrook these days, but we do our best to care for those who come our way."

Nathan nodded, not sure what to say. There was something in the reverend's voice that unsettled him—not in a bad way, but in a way that made him feel seen, as if the reverend could see through the layers of guilt and pain Nathan had buried beneath the surface.

"If you're looking for work, I could use some help fixing up the church," Reverend James continued. "It's seen better days, but with a little care, it could shine again."

Nathan glanced at the church, then back at the reverend. He felt the familiar urge to turn away, to keep moving, but something held him there. Maybe it was the weariness in his bones or the faint glimmer of hope that had been buried deep inside him for so long. Whatever it was, it made him say, "I can handle a hammer."

The reverend's smile widened. "Good. You can start tomorrow."

Chapter Two: A Town That Remains Still

The early light of dawn filtered through the cracked window of Nathan's small room at Riverside Boarding House. He lay there for a while, his body still heavy with the exhaustion of the long journey south. The bed beneath him creaked softly as he shifted, but the sound was soon drowned out by the quiet stirrings of the town waking up. He could hear the faint crowing of a rooster in the distance, the rhythmic clang of metal from Earl Wilson's blacksmith shop, and the faintest echo of children's laughter somewhere far off. It was strange—the town felt so small, so still—but there was life here, even if it was muted by the weight of the times. And it had been a long time since Nathan had been anywhere that felt like it was still alive.

He stared at the ceiling, his mind wandering as it often did in the quiet moments before the day began. The memories of New York crept in—the bustling streets, the noise, the speed of life. It had felt like the world had been moving too fast back then, spinning out of control. And when it finally crashed, it had taken everything from him.

Downstairs, Mrs. Helen Granger was bustling around the small kitchen, the smell of frying bacon and fresh coffee filling the room. Nathan entered the dining area, where a few other boarders were already seated, sipping from steaming mugs and quietly chatting. Mrs. Granger was a woman in her late 50s, her graying hair pulled into a tight bun at the back of her head. She had sharp blue eyes that missed nothing, and her no-nonsense demeanor made it clear that she ran the boarding house efficiently. Though she was firm, there was a warmth beneath her stern exterior—a kindness that revealed itself in the little things, like the extra slice of bacon she added to Nathan's plate without saying a word.

"Morning, Mr. Grant," she said as she returned to the stove. "Sleep well?"

Nathan gave a small nod, his response clipped. He was used to silence and people keeping their distance. But Mrs. Granger didn't seem to mind his lack of conversation. She'd seen plenty of men like him before—men who carried the weight of something too heavy to share.

As Nathan ate, Ryan Hayes strode in, full of energy despite the early hour. Ryan was a tall, lean young man in his late 20s with sandy blond hair that curled slightly at the edges. His green eyes sparkled with youthful optimism, and his hands were already stained with the blacksmith work he'd been doing early that morning.

"You must be the new guy," Ryan said with a grin, sitting down across from Nathan. "Heard you're helping the reverend fix up the church."

Nathan glanced up at the young man, noting the easy confidence in his posture. Ryan looked like someone the world hadn't yet worn down—someone who still believed things could improve.

"Yeah. For now," Nathan replied, keeping his answers brief. Ryan took a sip of his coffee, his grin never faltering.

"Reverend's a good man. Honest work, even if it's not much." He leaned back in his chair, stretching his long legs out in front of him. "You sticking around long?"

Nathan shrugged. "Depends."

Ryan's grin widened. "Well, if you're looking for more work, Earl's always saying he could use some help at the blacksmith shop. And there's Lillian Thompson over at Thompson Supplies. She's always got her hands full."

Later that morning, Nathan walked toward the small church that stood at the edge of town. The wooden building was old, its paint faded and peeling, with a steeple that looked like it hadn't been touched in years. But something about it felt sturdy like it had been standing through storm after storm and still hadn't fallen.

As he approached, Nathan saw Reverend James Matthews working on the fence. The reverend was tall, his shoulders broad but stooped slightly from years of manual labor. His hair was mostly gray, though a few streaks of black remained, and his deep-set brown eyes were kind but thoughtful, as though he saw more than he let on.

"Morning, Nathan," Reverend James greeted him, his voice warm and welcoming. "Ready to get to work?"

Nathan nodded, his eyes scanning the old church. "Looks like there's plenty to do."

Reverend James chuckled softly, wiping the sweat from his brow. "That's an understatement. But with a little hard work, this old place will shine again."

After leaving the church, Nathan found himself walking back through the center of town. The streets were still quiet, though the sun had climbed higher in the sky, casting long shadows across the buildings.

As he passed Thompson Supplies, he spotted Lillian Thompson outside, struggling with two large crates. Lillian was in her early 30s, with auburn hair that fell in loose waves around her face and striking blue eyes that stood out against her pale skin. There was a strength in how she carried herself, though it was clear that life had not been easy for her. She looked like someone who had been through her share of hardships but refused to let them break her.

Without thinking, Nathan stepped forward. "Need a hand?"

Lillian glanced up, surprised, but didn't hesitate to accept the help. "Thanks," she said, her voice soft but steady. "Wasn't expecting the delivery today."

As they carried the crates inside, Nathan noticed two small figures watching from behind the counter—Samuel and Grace, Lillian's children. At ten years old, Samuel already had the serious expression of someone much older. His brown hair was neatly combed, and his blue eyes, so much like his mother's, were filled with curiosity and caution. He watched Nathan closely as though trying to figure out what kind of man he was. Grace, just six years old, was the opposite of her brother. Her brown hair was messy from playing, and she clutched a small doll to her chest, her wide blue eyes filled with innocent curiosity. She gave Nathan a shy smile but stayed close to her brother.

"You've got some helpers," Nathan commented, setting the crate down. Lillian smiled, though there was a shadow of sadness in her expression. "They try to help where they can."

Nathan nodded, sensing the grief behind her words. He knew that look—he'd seen it in his reflection too many times. As he turned to leave, Grace stepped forward, her voice soft. "Thank you, mister."

Nathan paused, the sound of her voice tugging at something deep inside him. He gave a short nod before stepping outside, feeling the weight of the past pressing down on him once more.

That evening, as Nathan returned to Riverside Boarding House, the sky was painted in shades of orange and pink, the last rays of the sun casting long shadows across the town. The streets were mostly empty now, the people retreating to their homes as the chill of night settled in. Nathan's footsteps were slow as he walked, his thoughts drifting back to the people he had met that day—Reverend James, with his quiet wisdom; Ryan, with his easy laughter; and Lillian, with her strength and sadness. And the children. Samuel and Grace. Their faces lingered in his mind, reminding him too much of what he had lost.

As he reached the boarding house door, Nathan hesitated, his hand resting on the worn doorknob. For the first time in a long while, he felt the old urge to run. To leave before he let himself care too much.

But something about this town and its stillness made him pause. Maybe, he thought, just maybe, he could stay one more day.

Chapter Three: Roots of the Past

The morning sun filtered through the trees, casting dappled shadows on the dusty road as Nathan returned to the church. The air was cool, carrying the scent of wet earth and fresh grass, the kind of morning that might have felt peaceful if Nathan hadn't been carrying so much weight on his shoulders.

The town of Millbrook stirred gently in the distance, with smoke rising from chimneys and the faint hum of life echoing through the streets. It was quiet, as always, but there was a softness to the quiet—one that felt less suffocating than the endless silence Nathan had carried with him for years.

His footsteps slowed as he neared the church. He could already hear Reverend James Matthews working on the roof, hammering nails into the old, weathered wood. The reverend was a man who worked with his hands and who knew the value of patience and persistence. Something was comforting in the rhythm of the hammer, steady and unbroken.

As Nathan approached, Reverend James looked down from his perch, his brown eyes warm beneath the brim of his worn hat. "Morning, Nathan," he called, pausing in his work. "Thought you might be by early today."

Nathan nodded, glancing up at the reverend. "Figured I might as well start the day with some work."

"Well, there's no shortage of it here," the reverend said with a chuckle, hopping down from the roof with surprising agility for a man his age. "Come on, I've got a few boards that need replacing on the south side. Could use another pair of hands."

As they worked side by side, Nathan found the silence between them comfortable, the way it had been the day before. But Reverend James had a way of breaking the silence when it needed breaking—not with questions, but with quiet wisdom, as though he could sense what weighed on a man without being told.

"You've got a good hand with repairs," Reverend James said, watching Nathan measure a board before hammering it into place. "Ever do this kind of work before?"

Nathan nodded, his focus on the task at hand. "My father was a carpenter. Taught me everything I know about working with wood."

The reverend paused, studying Nathan for a moment. "Your father still around?"

Nathan hesitated, then shook his head. "Passed years ago. Pneumonia."

"I'm sorry to hear that," Reverend James said, his voice low but sincere. He didn't press for more, but Nathan could feel the reverend's eyes on him as if waiting for him to say something else.

Nathan cleared his throat, driving the hammer down on the nail with a sharp thud. "My mother passed not long after. Broken heart, I think."

Reverend James nodded slowly, the weight of Nathan's words hanging between them. "Grief has a way of breaking a person down," the reverend said softly. "But you've carried that weight for a long time, haven't you?"

Nathan didn't answer right away, his hands still working with the hammer, but his thoughts were elsewhere—on the past, his parents, Leslie, and Elizabeth. The weight had become a part of him, which clung to him no matter how far he ran.

"Some things are hard to shake," Nathan said quietly, almost to himself. Reverend James was silent for a moment, then placed a hand on Nathan's shoulder. "You don't have to carry it alone."

Nathan tensed at the touch but didn't pull away. He didn't know what to say to that, so he didn't say anything at all. Instead, he returned to the work, his mind swirling with thoughts he wasn't ready to confront.

After the morning's work, Nathan found himself wandering back through town. The streets were livelier now, with people moving about their daily routines—mothers with laundry baskets, men loading up wagons with supplies, and children playing near the town square. Something about the steady rhythm of life in Millbrook felt…different. People here moved with purpose, even in hard times, as though they had learned to hold on to whatever they could. Nathan's steps took him back to Thompson Supplies, almost without him realizing it. He wasn't sure what had drawn him back to the store, but as he approached, he saw Lillian Thompson standing outside, sorting through a stack of wooden crates.

Lillian looked up as Nathan approached, brushing a strand of auburn hair behind her ear. Her blue eyes, sharp but warm, met his with a brief flicker of surprise. "You're back," she said, her voice steady as always, though her tone had a note of curiosity.

Nathan nodded, his gaze moving to the crates. "Thought I might lend a hand."

Lillian hesitated, then smiled, though it didn't quite reach her eyes. "I could use the help."

They worked silently for a while, moving the crates into the store. The smell of sawdust and metal filled the air, and their footsteps echoed in the quiet space. Lillian moved with practiced efficiency, her hands quick and sure as she organized the stock.

Nathan couldn't help but admire her strength—a resilience about her, a quiet determination that reminded him of Leslie, though he quickly pushed the thought away. As they finished the last crate, Samuel and Grace appeared from the back of the store, their eyes lighting up when they saw Nathan.

"Mr. Grant!" Grace exclaimed, her small voice filled with excitement. She ran up to him, her brown hair bouncing as she clutched her doll tightly. "Are you here to help Mama again?"

Nathan smiled faintly, crouching down to her level. "Just giving her a hand." Standing a few feet behind his sister, Samuel crossed his arms, his expression serious. "We can help too, you know."

Nathan looked at the boy, seeing the same determination in his eyes as in Lillian's. "I'm sure you can," he said with a nod, rising to his feet.

Grace tugged at Nathan's sleeve, her wide blue eyes shining with curiosity. "Do you have a family, Mr. Grant?"

The question hit Nathan harder than he expected, and for a moment, he didn't know how to answer. His throat tightened, the weight of the past pressing down on him like a heavy stone.

Lillian's voice cut through the silence, her tone gentle but firm. "Grace, don't ask questions like that."

Grace's face fell, her small shoulders slumping. "I'm sorry…" Nathan forced a smile, though it felt hollow.

"It's okay," he said softly, his gaze moving to Lillian, who gave him a small, understanding nod.

Later that afternoon, Nathan was sitting on the porch outside Thompson Supplies, his mind churning with thoughts he wasn't ready to face. The town was quieter now, the sun beginning its slow descent toward the horizon, casting long shadows across the dusty road. The conversation with Grace still lingered in his mind, her innocent question opening old wounds he had tried so hard to bury. He hadn't talked about his family in years—not since he had lost them. And yet, here in Millbrook, surrounded by people who barely knew him, those old memories seemed to rise to the surface like ghosts that refused to stay buried.

Lillian stepped out onto the porch, wiping her hands on her apron. She hesitated momentarily, then sat beside Nathan, her gaze fixed on the horizon. "I'm sorry about Grace's question," Lillian said quietly. "She didn't mean to upset you."

Nathan shook his head, his eyes still on the road ahead. "It's not her fault." They sat silently for a moment, the weight of unspoken words hanging between them.

Lillian's voice was soft when she spoke again. "We've all lost something, Nathan. You don't have to talk about it, but… you don't have to carry it alone either."

Nathan turned to look at her, surprised by the echo of Reverend James's words. He hadn't expected kindness here or anyone to care about the burden he carried. But there was something in Lillian's eyes, something in the quiet strength of this town, that made him wonder if maybe…just maybe, he didn't have to keep running.

Chapter Four: Shadows of the Past

The room at Riverside Boarding House felt like a cage tonight, the walls pressing in on Nathan as he lay motionless on the small bed. His eyes traced the cracks in the ceiling, though his thoughts were far away, trapped in the endless loop of memories he had tried so hard to bury. Outside, the faint chirp of crickets and the rustling of the wind in the trees only served to amplify the stillness inside.

Sleep wouldn't come easily. It never did. Not with the weight of the past always pressing on him, not with the ghosts of those he had lost haunting his every thought. He turned over, willing his mind to quiet, but it was no use.

The moment he closed his eyes, the memories came flooding back—like a tidal wave, unstoppable and overwhelming.

Flashback: Elizabeth's Illness

He could hear the soft murmur of voices—the doctors, the nurses, their words clipped and clinical, but none of it had mattered. Nathan had been sitting by her bedside, watching his daughter's chest rise and fall in shallow, labored breaths. Elizabeth, his little girl. Her golden curls, now damp with fever, clung to her pale skin as she struggled to breathe. The pneumonia had taken hold of her so quickly, leaving her frail and weak, her once vibrant energy drained.

Nathan remembered how her hand had felt in his—so small, so fragile. He had tried to be strong for her, to keep his voice steady when he spoke, but the truth was, he had been falling apart inside. Every ragged breath she took felt like a countdown, like he was losing her, second by second.

Leslie had been there too, standing by the window, her arms wrapped tightly around herself as though she could somehow hold herself together. Her eyes were red from days of crying, and her body was tense with exhaustion and fear. Nathan had never seen her look so broken. She had always been the strong one—the one who kept their home warm and filled with laughter and never let life's hardships take away her smile. But in those final days, there had been no more smiles.

"Daddy…" Elizabeth's voice had been a faint whisper, barely audible over the rasp of her breath.

Nathan had leaned in close, forcing a smile he didn't feel. "I'm here, sweetheart. I'm right here."

Elizabeth's blue eyes had fluttered open, filled with a mix of trust and fear. She had believed in him—believed that he could make it all better like he always had. But this time, there was nothing he could do. No amount of money, no amount of pleading, could save her.

"I'm tired," she had whispered, her eyelids growing heavy. "I know," Nathan had said, his voice breaking as he squeezed her hand. "Just rest. I'll be here when you wake up."

But she hadn't woken up. By the time morning came, Elizabeth was gone, her small body still beneath the blankets, her once bright eyes forever closed.

Flashback: Leslie's Grief

The memory shifted, pulling Nathan further into the abyss. Elizabeth was gone, but the grief she left behind had seeped into every corner of their lives. The house had become a tomb filled with silence and sorrow.

Leslie had tried to keep going at first, tried to find some semblance of normalcy in the days that followed. But it was like the light inside her had been snuffed out. Nathan had thrown himself into his work, using it as a shield against the pain. The long hours at the office kept him from having to face the empty crib, the toys that Elizabeth would never play with again. He had buried himself in numbers, stocks, and deals—anything to keep his mind occupied or from thinking about what he had lost.

But Leslie… she hadn't been able to bury the pain. It had consumed her, eating away at her spirit until there was nothing left but an empty shell of the woman she had once been. Nathan remembered how she had looked at him one night, standing in the kitchen with her hands gripping the edge of the counter, her eyes hollow.

"Do you even care anymore?" she had asked, her voice trembling with emotion. "Do you even feel anything?"

Nathan had stared at her, the words catching in his throat. He had felt everything—too much. The weight of it had been crushing him, but he hadn't known how to express it. So he had turned away, using work as an escape.

"You're never here," Leslie had said, her voice cracking. "You're shutting me out."

"I'm doing this for us," Nathan had snapped, though even as he said the words, they had felt like a lie. "I'm trying to fix this."

"Fix what?" Leslie had demanded, her eyes filling with tears. "You can't fix this, Nathan. She's gone. She's gone, and you're not here."

Nightmare: Leslie's Death

The flashback twisted into a familiar nightmare—one that Nathan had been running from for years. It was always the same: night, rain, and the slick pavement of New York's streets glistening under the dim glow of streetlights.

He walked through the rain, his shoes splashing in the puddles, his coat soaked through. He had been working late again. Another argument with Leslie that morning, another long day at the office where he had buried himself in paperwork to avoid the suffocating grief at home.

But when he turned the corner, the nightmare always hit him like a blow to the chest—the wreckage. Red and blue lights flashed in the rain-soaked street, illuminating the mangled car that had slammed into the lamppost. His breath caught in his throat as he ran toward it, his heart pounding in his ears, his chest tight with fear.

"Leslie!" Nathan shouted, his voice hoarse with panic. "Leslie!"

The paramedics were already there, their faces grim as they worked to pull her from the wreckage. But Nathan knew. He knew the moment he saw her pale, lifeless body. He had failed her. The grief, the guilt, crashed over him in waves, pulling him under. He hadn't been there for her. Not when she needed him most.

Waking Up: The Weight of Guilt

Nathan jolted awake, his chest heaving as he gasped for air. The dark room felt suffocating, the walls too close, the air too thick. His heart raced in his chest, the familiar panic of the nightmare clinging to him like a second skin.

For a moment, he didn't know where he was—his mind still trapped in the nightmare, still back on that rain-soaked street. But as his eyes adjusted to the darkness, the familiar surroundings of Riverside Boarding House came into focus.

He was in Millbrook. The wreckage was gone. Leslie was gone.

But the guilt… the guilt was still heavy and suffocating as ever. He sat up in bed, running a trembling hand through his damp hair. His shirt clung to his skin, soaked with sweat, and his breath came in short, shallow gasps. The memories had been relentless tonight—Elizabeth's death, Leslie's accident. The weight of both losses pressed down on him, making it hard to breathe. He hadn't been able to save either of them. His daughter, taken by pneumonia, and his wife, lost in a car wreck that should have never happened. And the worst part—the part that haunted him every day—was knowing that his last words to Leslie had been spoken in anger. "I'm trying to fix this." But he hadn't fixed anything. He had only made it worse.

The first light of dawn began to creep through the thin curtains, casting a faint glow across the room. Nathan sat on the edge of the bed, staring at the sliver of light, his mind still foggy with the remnants of the nightmare.

Outside, the town of Millbrook was beginning to wake, the early morning sounds of birds chirping and the rustle of trees breaking through the silence. But inside, Nathan felt none of the peace the town seemed to offer.

His past clung to him like a shadow, always there, reminding him of what he had lost. And no matter how far he ran or how many towns he passed through, the weight of that guilt followed him. It had been years since Elizabeth and Leslie were taken from him, but the pain was still as raw as it had been on the day he lost them.

Nathan pressed his hands to his face, the exhaustion settling deep into his bones. How much longer could he carry this? How long could he keep running from something that is always with him?

As the sun rose higher, Nathan knew he couldn't stay in the room any longer. The walls felt like they were closing in, the air too thick to breathe. He needed to move, walk, clear his head—anything to escape the suffocating weight of his memories. He threw on his coat and stepped out into the cool morning air without bothering to wash up. The sky was painted in soft pink and orange hues, the peaceful dawn that might have given him hope once—before everything had fallen apart.

Chapter Five: A Quiet Morning

Nathan walked through the quiet streets of Millbrook, his footsteps echoing in the stillness. The town had an almost ethereal quality in the early morning light, bathed in soft pinks and oranges that stretched across the horizon. Smoke curled lazily from the chimneys of a few houses, and the smell of wood and damp earth filled the air. Nathan's breath came out in short puffs, visible in the cool air as he walked, each step heavy with the memories that still clung to him from the night.

The town was quiet and peaceful, but there was no peace inside him. The restless, gnawing guilt lingered like an old wound that refused to heal, and every building, every street seemed like just another place where he didn't belong. His mind raced with questions—ones he didn't want to face but couldn't escape. Why had he survived when Leslie and Elizabeth hadn't? What had he done to deserve to keep breathing, when the two people he loved most had been taken from him?

He walked past the church, its weathered steeple reaching toward the sky, and for a brief moment, Nathan felt a flicker of something deep inside him. It wasn't peace—he was far from finding that—but it was a glimmer of... something. Hope? He wasn't sure. He wasn't even sure if he believed in hope anymore. But the sight of the church, standing tall despite the years of neglect, stirred something in him that he couldn't quite name. He kept walking, passing the blacksmith's shop, where the rhythmic clang of metal rang out even this early in the morning.

Earl Wilson, the town's blacksmith, was already hard at work, his strong arms swinging the hammer with a steady rhythm that seemed to echo through the air. Nathan's feet carried him toward Thompson Supplies, though he hadn't intended to go there. It was as if his body moved of its own accord, drawn to the familiarity of the place or perhaps to the people inside. He slowed as he approached, his gaze falling on the weathered wooden sign above the door, the sun casting long shadows across the building.

He hadn't spoken much to Lillian Thompson since he had helped her with the crates the other day, but something about her—about how she carried her burdens with quiet strength—had stayed with him. She was still grieving, too, though she didn't show it outwardly. He recognized the look in her eyes, the way she held herself together for her children, even when the weight of her sorrow threatened to crush her.

Nathan stopped just outside the store, hesitating for a moment. He saw Samuel and Grace through the window, the two children playing quietly by the counter. Samuel's face was serious as always, his young eyes already too old for his years. Grace, with her messy hair and wide eyes, was laughing softly as she held her doll close, unaware of the deep sadness that filled the adults around her. For a brief moment, he wondered what his life would have been like if Elizabeth had lived. Would she have grown up to be like Grace? Would she have laughed and played, blissfully unaware of the world's harshness?

The thought twisted something deep inside him, a pang of sorrow so sharp it nearly took his breath away. Before he could think twice, the door to the store opened, and Lillian stepped outside, wiping her hands on her apron. She looked up, startled to see him there, but quickly recovered, offering him a small smile.

"Nathan," she said softly, her voice still carrying the warmth he had come to associate with her. "You're out early."

Nathan nodded, glancing at the children inside the store before looking back at her. "Couldn't sleep," he admitted.

Lillian studied him for a moment, her blue eyes searching his face. She didn't ask him why he couldn't sleep—she didn't need to. She understood the weight of sleepless nights, the way grief and guilt kept a person awake long after the world had gone quiet.

"I was just about to make some coffee," she said after a moment, gesturing toward the door. "You're welcome to join us if you'd like."

Nathan hesitated, his instinct still telling him to keep his distance and to walk away before he let himself get too close to these people and let himself care. But the thought of being alone with his memories, with the ghosts of Leslie and

Elizabeth, was more than he could bear. He nodded once, stepping toward the door as Lillian held it open for him.

Inside, the store's warmth washed over him, a welcome contrast to the cold air outside. The smell of fresh coffee brewing filled the small space, and for the first time in a long while, Nathan felt a faint sense of comfort—if only for a moment.

Grace looked up from her doll and smiled brightly when she saw him. "Mr. Grant!" she exclaimed, her voice filled with childlike excitement. "Mama says you helped us last time!"

Nathan managed a small smile, though the effort felt heavy. "Just a little," he said, glancing at Lillian as she busied herself with the coffee.

Samuel, ever the serious one, stood quietly by the counter, his arms crossed over his chest as he watched Nathan with a thoughtful gaze. "You staying in Millbrook long?" he asked, his tone neutral but filled with curiosity.

Nathan didn't know how to answer that. He didn't know if he could stay—if he could even stay in one place for too long without the weight of his past crushing him. But something about this town, about these people, made him want to try. Made him want to believe, if only for a moment, that maybe he didn't have to keep running.

"I don't know," he said honestly, meeting the boy's gaze. "I guess we'll see."

Samuel nodded, accepting the answer without question, though his young face remained serious. "I think you should stay," he said quietly. "Mama says you're a good man."

The words hit Nathan harder than he expected, the simple honesty of a child cutting through the layers of guilt and shame he had wrapped himself in for years. A good man. He hadn't felt like a good man in a long time, not since the day he had lost everything. But as he looked at Samuel and then at Grace, who was still watching him with wide, hopeful eyes, he felt a flicker of something inside him—something he hadn't felt in years. Maybe, just maybe, there was a way forward.

The rich and inviting smell of coffee filled the room, but Nathan couldn't fully enjoy it. His mind was still tangled in the mess of thoughts from the early morning, and the images of Leslie and Elizabeth flashed through his mind quickly. Their faces, their laughter, and the sound of Elizabeth's small voice calling out to him haunted him.

Lillian handed him a cup of coffee, her eyes softening when she noticed the faraway look in his eyes. "You've been through a lot," she said quietly, her voice gentle but steady.

Nathan wrapped his hands around the warm cup, but he didn't respond. What could he say? Lillian had her losses, her pain, and yet she stood here every day, working, caring for her children, carrying her grief with a quiet dignity that

Nathan admired but didn't understand. "You don't have to carry it alone, you know," she added after a moment, her eyes never leaving his.

Nathan swallowed hard, the weight of her words settling deep inside him. He hadn't talked to anyone about Leslie or Elizabeth in years. He didn't know if he could. But standing here, in this small store, surrounded by the warmth of Lillian and her children, he felt the smallest crack in the walls he had built around himself. Maybe, just maybe, he didn't have to carry it alone.

Chapter Six: Beneath the Surface

Lillian stood at the kitchen counter in the back of Thompson Supplies, her hands moving methodically as she cleaned the few dishes from breakfast. The store had been quiet all morning except for the occasional clatter from Samuel or Grace in the front, their muffled voices filling the silence behind her. Yet her mind wasn't on the present—it rarely was these days. It was constantly drifting back to what had been, to the memories she both cherished and dreaded.

The sound of running water filled the small space, the warm steam rising from the sink and fogging the window above her. Lillian wiped her hands on her apron, staring out at the backyard, still dusted with the remnants of frost from the previous chilly night. The cold seeped into everything lately. She could feel it in her bones and heart as if the warmth she had once known had been buried long ago. Her fingers stilled for a moment, gripping the edge of the counter as she allowed herself a brief moment of weakness.

Henry.

His name came unbidden into her mind, the weight of his absence pressing down on her like it always did, like it always would. She had learned how to live without him, but there were moments—like this one—when she still felt as if a piece of her had been ripped away.

Three years ago. It had been the height of summer, the sun hot in the Tennessee sky, the air heavy with the smell of dry grass and wildflowers. The children had been outside, running barefoot through the fields, their laughter echoing through the warm air.

Henry had been in the store, fixing one of the shelves that had come loose in the back. She could still picture him, his brown hair streaked with sweat, his strong hands working with the kind of practiced ease from years of doing the same task. They had always worked side by side. When they first opened the store together, it had felt like a dream—a shared vision of what their life could be. Henry had built the shelves himself, and every board and nail was placed with care as if each piece was a testament to the life they were building.

Lillian managed the front, ensuring the stock was in order and the customers left with what they needed. Together, they had created something that felt permanent, a foundation for their family. But that foundation had crumbled the day Henry collapsed. The heat had been stifling that day, the kind of oppressive heat that made it hard to breathe. Lillian had been outside with the children, watching them as they played in the yard, their laughter a constant background noise to the rhythm of the store.

It had been a good day—normal, steady, just like so many others. Then she heard the crash. At first, she thought something was falling in the store—maybe one of the shelves had come loose again, or a customer had knocked something over. But when she walked inside, the sight that greeted her was something she had never expected. Henry was on the floor, his face pale, his hand clutching his chest. His eyes were wide with panic, his breaths coming in short, labored gasps. "Henry!" Lillian had cried, rushing to his side, her heart racing with fear. "Henry, what's happening?"

He couldn't answer. He had tried to speak, but the words wouldn't come. His body was failing him, and there was nothing she could do to stop it. She had called for help, her voice frantic as she held him, her hands shaking as she tried to keep him with her. But by the time the doctor arrived, it was too late. Henry was gone, his once strong, capable body lying still on the floor of the store they had built together.

The memory hit her with the same force now as it had that day, and Lillian gripped the edge of the sink harder, the pain raw and sharp. She had been alone since then, raising Samuel and Grace by herself, keeping the store afloat with little more than sheer willpower. It wasn't easy, but she had no choice. There was no one else to help, no one else to lean on. She had learned to be strong, to carry the weight of it all on her shoulders. But the weight was heavy, and there were moments like this when it felt unbearable.

The nights were the worst. The silence would settle over the house, the absence of Henry's presence like a void that stretched across every room. She would lie awake, staring at the ceiling, listening to the sound of her children breathing in the next room, their innocent sleep so peaceful. And she would wonder how she was supposed to do it—how she was supposed to raise them without him and be both mother and father, both comforter and protector.

She had learned to push through, keep moving, and focus on the tasks. But sometimes, in the quiet moments, the grief would rise up like a wave, threatening to pull her under. She couldn't afford to drown in it—not when her children needed her. So she had built walls around her heart, just enough to keep the pain at bay, just enough to survive.

She was pulled from her thoughts by the sound of footsteps approaching. Nathan. She had seen the look in his eyes this morning, the way his shoulders carried that invisible weight she knew all too well. She recognized it because she wore it, too, day in and day out—the weight of grief, loss, and the relentless ache that never fully healed.

She turned just as he entered the small kitchen area, his footsteps slow and deliberate as if he wasn't sure whether he belonged there.

"You're working too hard," Nathan said, his voice low but firm.

There was a gentleness to his words, though—a concern she hadn't expected from someone who had barely begun to let himself feel anything. Lillian wiped her hands on her apron and smiled, though it didn't reach her eyes.

"It's what keeps me going," she replied, returning to the dishes. "There's always work to be done."

Nathan nodded, stepping further into the room. He leaned against the doorframe, watching her silently for a moment as if he was trying to understand something about her—something she wasn't ready to share.

"I know what it's like," he said quietly, breaking the silence. "To lose someone."

Lillian stilled, her fingers tightening around the dishcloth in her hands. She hadn't expected him to say that. She sensed something deeper in Nathan, something dark and unresolved, but he had never spoken about it until now.

She turned slowly, her blue eyes meeting his dark ones. "How did you...?"

Nathan looked down, his jaw tightening as if struggling to find the right words. "My wife and daughter," he said, his voice rough. "I lost them both."

The air in the room seemed still, the weight of his confession hanging between them like a heavy curtain. Lillian's heart ached at the raw pain in his voice, the way his eyes darkened with memories he clearly hadn't shared with anyone else.

She understood that pain. She understood it far too well. "I'm sorry," she whispered, the words feeling inadequate.

But what else could she say? There was no way to truly comfort someone who had been through that kind of loss. She knew that better than anyone.

Nathan's eyes flicked back up to hers, and for a brief moment, they stood there in shared silence, two people who had been broken by life, carrying wounds that would never fully heal.

"Sometimes," Nathan continued, his voice softer now, "I wonder if it'll ever stop hurting. If there's a way to... move on."

Lillian set the dishcloth down, stepping closer to him. "You don't move on," she said, her voice steady but filled with emotion. "You carry it with you, every day. But you learn to live with it."

Nathan's gaze softened, and he nodded slowly, though his eyes were still uncertain. He wasn't sure if he believed that yet or if he could ever learn to live with the weight of his past.

Lillian turned back to the sink, her thoughts drifting once again to Henry, to the years they had shared before it all came crashing down. She had learned to live without him, but the pain of losing him never left. It was always there, beneath the surface, waiting for quiet moments like this to rise up and remind her of what she had lost.

"I think about him all the time," she admitted softly, surprising even herself with the confession.

She rarely spoke about Henry, even to the children. It was easier to keep those memories locked away, to focus on the present instead of the past. But something about Nathan made her feel like she didn't have to hide it. Nathan remained silent, listening, waiting for her to continue.

"He was everything to me," Lillian continued, her voice trembling slightly. "And then he was gone, just like that. One minute, he was right here, and the next…" She trailed off, her throat tightening with emotion.

She didn't finish the sentence. She didn't need to. Nathan understood.

The warmth of the kitchen felt stifling now, thick with unspoken words and unresolved pain. Lillian stepped back from the sink, wiping her hands on her apron once more, trying to steady herself. The memories of Henry weighed heavily on her, but there was something about sharing that weight with Nathan, however briefly, that lightened the burden—if only for a moment.

Nathan hadn't moved from his spot by the door, but his gaze was softer now, his usual guarded expression lessened. There was an understanding between them, something unspoken but undeniable. They were two people with the same kind of grief, though their stories differed. For a long moment, neither of them spoke.

The quiet of the kitchen wrapped around them, and outside, the muffled sounds of Samuel and Grace playing filled the small space, reminding Lillian of her reason for pushing forward every day. She had to keep going—for them. But sometimes, she wondered how much longer she could keep it up, how much longer she could shoulder the weight alone.

"I don't talk about him much," Lillian finally said, breaking the silence. Her voice was quieter now, almost a whisper. "Not even to the children. They were so young when it happened… I don't think they fully understand what it meant to lose him."

Nathan's brow furrowed slightly as he watched her, his dark eyes filled with empathy. "Maybe that's why you should talk about him," he said gently. "They might not understand now, but they'll need to know. They'll need to understand who he was—who their father was."

Lillian's chest tightened at his words. He was right, of course, but it wasn't easy to talk about Henry. Not when the pain was still so fresh, so raw. But Nathan's words lingered in her mind, planting a seed of thought she hadn't considered before. She had been trying to protect Samuel and Grace from the full weight of the loss, but maybe they needed to know more. Maybe they needed to hear about their father from her—before the memories became too faded, too distant.

"I just don't want to burden them," Lillian admitted, her voice breaking slightly. "They've already lost so much. I don't want them to feel… weighed down by the past."

Nathan shook his head slowly, stepping forward just enough to close the gap between them. "Talking about it won't burden them," he said softly. "It'll help them remember. And it'll help you, too. Trust me, I know how hard it is to carry it all inside."

Lillian met his gaze again, feeling the sincerity in his words. She knew he was right. She had been holding onto Henry's memories, afraid to let them out and afraid of what it would do to her if she spoke about him aloud. But maybe, just maybe, sharing those memories with her children and Nathan would help her heal, even if only a little. She sighed a long, deep breath that seemed to release some of the tension she had been holding.

"I'll think about it," she said, her voice steadier now. "Maybe it's time."

Nathan nodded, his expression softening even further. "You don't have to do it all at once," he said, offering her a small, understanding smile. "One step at a time."

Lillian returned the smile, though it was faint. "Thank you," she said quietly. "I didn't expect to… talk about this today."

"I didn't expect to either," Nathan replied, his voice carrying a hint of warmth that hadn't been there before.

"But I'm glad we did."

For the first time in what felt like ages, Lillian felt a sense of lightness. It wasn't overwhelming, and it wasn't permanent, but it was there—a small flicker of relief in the midst of the storm she had been carrying for so long. Sharing her grief with Nathan, even in that small way, had made it feel less suffocating.

She glanced at the door, where the sounds of Samuel and Grace playing outside filtered in once more. "I should check on the children," she said, her voice still soft but more assured now. "But if you ever need to talk, Nathan... about your wife, about your daughter... I'm here."

Nathan's eyes softened, and for a moment, he looked like he might say something in return. But instead, he nodded, his expression a mixture of gratitude and something deeper—something that lingered in the space between them.

"Thank you," he said, his voice thick with emotion. "I'll remember that."

As Lillian stepped outside, the crisp morning air hit her skin, waking her from the heaviness of the kitchen. Samuel and Grace were running around the yard, their laughter ringing as they chased each other in circles. For a moment, she stood there, watching them, feeling a sense of bittersweet joy. They were so young, so full of life, and yet they had already experienced so much loss.

Nathan followed her, standing beside her as they watched the children. The warmth of the sun had started to melt the frost that still lingered on the grass, and Lillian felt the cool air brushing against her skin, a welcome change from the warmth of the store.

"They remind me of Elizabeth," Nathan said quietly, his voice so soft that Lillian almost didn't hear him. Lillian turned to him, her brow furrowed in understanding.

"Your daughter?" Nathan nodded, his gaze still fixed on the children. "She was about Grace's age when… when we lost her. She had the same kind of laugh. The kind that fills a room."

Lillian's heart ached at his words, and his voice broke slightly when he spoke about Elizabeth. It was the first time he had spoken about his daughter since their earlier conversation, and Lillian could feel the weight of those memories in the air between them.

"She sounds like she was a beautiful child," Lillian said softly.

"She was," Nathan replied, his voice distant. "I think about her every day. And Leslie… I think about them both. Sometimes, I still carry them with me, even though they're gone."

Lillian nodded, understanding that feeling all too well. "I think we carry the people we've lost with us forever," she said. "They never really leave us. They stay in our hearts, in our memories. And sometimes, that's all we have to hold onto."

Nathan turned to look at her then, his dark eyes filled with emotion. For a long moment, they stood there, two people bound by grief, loss, and the shared understanding that some wounds never fully heal.

But in that moment, Lillian realized they might not have to heal completely. Maybe it was enough to carry the memories, to remember the love, and to find some peace in the process. As Samuel and Grace's laughter filled the air again, Lillian smiled faintly, the weight on her chest feeling a little lighter.

Chapter Seven: A Town's Heartbeat

Nathan leaned his weight into the hammer, driving the nail deeper into the worn wood of the church's entrance. His breath puffed out in white clouds in the chilly morning air, and the weight of the past few days pressed on his shoulders like an invisible burden.

Reverend James had asked for help repairing the church's roof, and while Nathan wasn't one to join community efforts easily, he found himself accepting the offer. Work kept his hands busy, which was better than the alternative—being trapped in his thoughts. The church itself, like the rest of Millbrook, bore the scars of the economic collapse caused by the Great Depression.

The once-vibrant white paint was peeling from the walls, leaving patches of exposed wood that had begun to weather and crack. The windows were unevenly patched with panes of glass donated by the townsfolk, some too small and others mismatched in color. The steeple, once a symbol of hope, now sagged slightly, its frame weakened by years of neglect. Funds were scarce. Every dollar was stretched thin, and every repair was postponed until it became critical. Even the benches inside the church were worn, with sagging cushions and chipped wood.

The townspeople attended Sunday services faithfully, but there was an underlying heaviness to their worship now—one shaped by fear and uncertainty for the future. People held on to their faith, but it was clear that faith alone couldn't fill their empty bellies or fix their crumbling homes. Reverend James appeared around the corner, his face lined with fatigue but his eyes warm as he looked at Nathan's work. His overcoat, though well-kept, was threadbare at the seams, a visible sign of the times.

"You've got a good hand with tools," the reverend said, his voice rough from years of preaching to a town that had grown too used to hardship. "This roof's been needing fixing for a while now."

Nathan nodded, wiping the sweat from his brow, though the cold morning made it unnecessary. "Happy to help," he said, though the words felt foreign in his mouth. He hadn't felt part of a community in so long—maybe not since Leslie and Elizabeth.

The reverend smiled faintly, though his face remained tired. "These days, we take all the help we can get. It's been hard on everyone—some more than others." His eyes wandered down the street, where several townspeople passed by. Nathan knew what he meant.

The Great Depression had been cruel to the people of Millbrook. Farms had been foreclosed, families displaced, and jobs lost. The town's spirit had changed, yet a glimmer of resilience was still in the air. People weren't giving up, at least not yet.

Nathan lowered his gaze, focusing on his work again, the rhythmic pounding of the hammer grounding him. "It's hard everywhere," he said after a moment, his voice low. "This isn't the first place I've seen like this."

Reverend James watched Nathan for a moment, his brow furrowed as though he wanted to say more, but instead, he gave a quiet nod. "I reckon you've seen your share of hard times, too," he said quietly. "These days, it's hard for anyone to find their footing."

Nathan didn't respond immediately, but his hands were still working on the repairs. But the reverend's words rang true. He had seen more than his share of hardship, but this wasn't just about him. Everywhere he looked, the town was worn down by the same relentless grind of the Great Depression.

People were losing their homes and their jobs. Families struggled to put food on the table. It was a quiet despair that didn't always show on the surface but lingered in every conversation. Glances are exchanged between neighbors.

Reverend James stepped closer, his tone softening. "The town's hurting, but folks here—they lean on each other. Even in times like this, we find a way to pull together. You'll see." Nathan glanced up, meeting the reverend's gaze. There was a kind of tired hope in the man's eyes, a belief that despite everything, they could endure. It was a hope that Nathan wasn't sure he could share—not yet.

After finishing his work at the church, Nathan made his way down the main street. The town of Millbrook, like so many others across the country, had been hit hard by the Great Depression. The once-bustling shops were quiet now, their windows dark, some boarded up. Smith's Hardware only opened its doors three days a week now, and the stock inside was thin. People couldn't afford to buy new tools or new supplies, not when they barely had enough to buy food.

As he walked past Frank's Groceries, he noticed the sign on the door: Bread, butter, and coffee rationed. It wasn't the first time he'd seen the sign, but it reminded him of how desperate things had become each time. The shelves inside were sparsely stocked, and Frank, the shopkeeper, had taken to selling what little he could get his hands on. Bags of flour were smaller now, and canned goods were hard to come by. Frank's face had grown more gaunt over the months, the constant strain of keeping the store running visible in the deep lines etched across his forehead.

Across the street, a group of men stood by the closed doors of the blacksmith's shop. Their hats were pulled low over their brows, their coats worn and frayed at the edges. They spoke quietly, their voices heavy with the weight of worry. Earl Wilson, the blacksmith, leaned against the side of the building, his hands blackened with soot. He hadn't had much work lately. People weren't spending money on repairs they couldn't afford, and even the farmers who needed their tools fixed were bartering now—trading food, labor, or whatever they could spare instead of cash. Nathan's stomach twisted as he watched them.

It reminded him of his time in New York—how quickly everything could be lost, how fragile life was. The stock market had crashed, and it felt like the world had ended. For many, it had. Men who had once worked in factories, farms, or offices now wandered the streets, looking for any scrap of work they could find. A pang of guilt shot through Nathan. He had been one of those men once—lost and desperate, wondering how he would rebuild his life.

But unlike the men in Millbrook, he had left everything behind. He had run, hoping to find peace somewhere along the way. Now, watching the town struggle, he wondered if staying would have been better—if facing his pain head-on was the only way ever truly to heal.

Back at Thompson Supplies, Lillian was dealing with her own struggles. Samuel had been quiet lately—too quiet. He didn't complain, but she could see the frustration building in him, the way he clenched his fists when things didn't go right. He had started to grow into his father's shoes, but the weight of those shoes was too heavy for him. Samuel had taken to helping more around the store, but it wasn't enough to keep his mind occupied. He missed Henry—the way his father had always been there, teaching and guiding him.

With the pressure of the times pressing down on them, Lillian feared that Samuel was withdrawing further into himself, bottling up emotions that needed to be released. That afternoon, as she organized the store's limited supplies, she noticed Samuel sitting by the counter, staring at a book before him but not reading it. His brow was furrowed, his jaw set. He looked so much like Henry in that moment that Lillian had to pause, the familiar ache in her chest returning.

"Samuel," she said softly, walking over to him. "Is something bothering you?"

Samuel didn't look up at first, but after a moment, he shrugged. "I just… don't see the point of school anymore," he mumbled. "It doesn't matter. Everything's broken. No one will care if I get good grades when no jobs are left."

The words hit Lillian hard. She knew he was right in some ways. The world had become a different place, a harsher place. But she couldn't bear the thought of Samuel giving up, losing hope like so many others.

"School still matters," she said firmly, though her voice was gentle. "Your education is something no one can take from you, even when everything else is uncertain. We'll get through this, Samuel. But we have to keep trying."

Samuel glanced up at her then, his eyes filled with frustration that went deeper than school. "I miss him, Mama," he whispered, his voice breaking. "I miss him so much."

Lillian felt her throat tighten, but she knelt in front of him, placing her hand on his. "I miss him too," she whispered back. "Every day. But we have to keep going. We have to be strong, for each other."

Chapter Eight: Beneath a Quiet Sky

Later that day, Nathan found himself at the small gathering Lillian had mentioned—a picnic held in the open field behind the weathered church. Despite the pervasive hardships of the Great Depression, the townspeople had come together, offering what little food they could spare. There were no grand feasts, just simple meals of bread, beans, and a few vegetables from their fading gardens. Yet, even with such humble offerings, the gathering held a sense of community and warmth that transcended scarcity. This shared resilience made the gathering feel rich in spirit, if not in material things.

Nathan stood at the edge of the field at first, unsure. He wasn't used to being part of something like this anymore. Events like this—the laughter, the shared food, the easy companionship—used to be a regular part of his life before everything had unraveled. Now, they only reminded him of all he had lost. It felt like stepping into a world he no longer belonged to, a world he had deliberately left behind.

Yet, something had drawn him here today. Maybe it was the kindness in Lillian's invitation, or maybe it was the quiet pull of something he hadn't been able to name until now. From his spot at the edge of the gathering, Nathan watched children race around the field, their laughter ringing like a joyful song amidst the weariness. Their clothes were worn thin, patches hastily sewn over the knees and elbows, and their shoes were little more than scraps of leather barely holding together. But none of that seemed to matter at that moment. Their faces were bright with childhood innocence, untouched by their parents' struggles. Their joy was real, unburdened, and for a fleeting moment, Nathan found himself smiling faintly, remembering the days when his own daughter, Elizabeth, had laughed like that.

The adults stood in small clusters, talking in low voices. Their faces were lined with the marks of hardship—worry etched deep into their features—but there was something else there, too. In the way they leaned toward each other and shared stories and small bits of food, there was a quiet determination, a refusal to let the crushing weight of the times take everything from them. They had lost much, but they still had each other, and that was a kind of wealth no amount of money could buy.

Lillian spotted Nathan standing at the edge and waved him over with a welcoming smile. She was standing with Reverend James and a few other townsfolk, holding a small plate of food. It was a modest meal—just bread, beans, and a few roasted vegetables—but there was a grace in its simplicity, as though each bite carried more than sustenance.

"Glad you came," Lillian said warmly as he approached. "We don't have much, but it's something."

Nathan hesitated for a moment before taking the plate she offered. "Thank you," he murmured, his voice quiet, but there was a softness in his tone that hadn't been there before.

He looked down at the food—humble but prepared with care—and realized it was more than a meal. It was a gesture, an invitation into their world and community. It was something he hadn't realized he'd been missing.

As he stood with the group, the scent of the warm bread and beans rose to meet him, mingling with the crisp autumn air. The sun was starting to lower, casting a golden light across the field, and in that moment, its simplicity all struck him. He hadn't felt this kind of quiet contentment in years. Not since before… everything.

Reverend James stepped forward, his plate in hand, and smiled as he looked around at the gathering. "Folks here don't have much," he said, his voice carrying the roughness of years spent preaching to a tired congregation. "But we've got heart. That's what'll get us through. We may not be rich in money, but we're rich in spirit. That's worth more than any dollar these days."

Nathan glanced around again, seeing the way the townspeople interacted. There was a gentleness in how they passed food to each other, a kind of unspoken understanding that they were all together. The children's laughter, the adults' quiet conversations, and the way people lingered despite the evening chill—it all painted a picture of something Nathan hadn't experienced in a long time. Community. Belonging.

Nathan was drawn into conversations with the men nearby as the sun dipped lower, casting long shadows over the field. Rough hands that bore the marks of manual labor gestured as they spoke of small jobs they had picked up around town—repairing fences, patching roofs, cutting firewood for the coming winter.

One of the men, a tall farmer named Earl, mentioned they could use another set of hands. Nathan wasn't sure what made him hesitate. He had kept to himself for so long, moving from town to town, job to job, never settling. The idea of staying in one place, of putting down roots again, felt foreign. But something in the man's offer—how these men welcomed him without question—made him pause. It felt like a small invitation, not just to work but to be part of something again.

"I'll think about it," Nathan said, his voice careful but sincere. It wasn't a promise, but it wasn't a refusal either. And that, for now, was enough.

As the evening wore on, the picnic began to wind down. The children's laughter grew softer as they tired, and families packed up their blankets and baskets one by one, preparing to head home. Nathan sat on a wooden bench at the edge of the field, watching as the last of the day's light faded into dusk.

Lillian joined him, sitting beside him quietly as she watched her own children—Samuel and Grace—play one last game before it was time to leave. Her presence was serene, a calm strength Nathan had recognized. She didn't fill the silence with unnecessary words. Instead, she simply sat with him, sharing the stillness.

"I wasn't sure you'd come," she admitted softly after a moment, her voice so quiet it was almost lost in the rustle of the wind through the trees. "But I'm glad you did."

Nathan turned to look at her, his gaze meeting hers for a long moment. "I wasn't sure either," he replied honestly. "But… I think I needed to."

Lillian smiled, a soft, understanding smile, and nodded. They sat together for a while longer, watching as the town slowly emptied. The warmth of the moment, the shared understanding between them, was enough. It wasn't a resolution—not yet—but it was a step forward. And sometimes, that was all a person needed.

As the last of the townspeople made their way home, Nathan lingered behind, walking slowly through the now-empty field. The moon had risen, casting a pale, silver light over the town, and the streets of Millbrook were quiet once more. The children's laughter and the quiet hum of conversation had faded into the night, leaving behind a peaceful stillness.

He passed by the church, where the repairs he had worked on earlier in the week stood in contrast to the weathered structure. It wasn't much, but it was something—a small mark of progress, a sign that things could still be mended even in the midst of hardship.

As he returned to the Riverside Boarding House, Nathan paused by the Willowbend River, which ran just behind the property. The sound of the water moving over smooth stones filled the air, the gentle current reflecting the moon's soft glow. The river had always been there, steady and quiet, offering a sense of calm that Nathan hadn't realized he needed.

He knelt by the riverbank, dipping his hand into the cool water, feeling the familiar sensation as it flowed over his skin. It reminded him of the rivers back home, where he and Elizabeth used to spend their summers. They had skipped rocks, laughing as the small stones plopped into the current. The memory, once too painful to bear, now felt softened by time. There was still sadness there, but it wasn't as sharp as it once had been. It had become part of him, woven into the fabric of who he was.

The river's steady flow seemed to mirror the quiet resilience of Millbrook—both moving forward, even when the world around them felt like it was falling apart. As Nathan stood by the water's edge, watching the current, he felt a faint pull toward something new beyond his reach. The river, like Millbrook, had endured. And maybe, just maybe, he could too.

With one last look at the river, Nathan turned and returned to the boarding house. The soft rush of the water followed him, a gentle hum that seemed to echo in the quiet night. As he stepped inside, closing the door behind him, he realized—for the first time in years—that perhaps, he might be ready to belong somewhere again.

Chapter Nine: In the Shadow of Doubt

Nathan's hands gripped the axe handle, each swing landing with a satisfying thud as it split the logs in front of him. The repetitive motion, the sheer force behind each strike, helped keep the rising storm of his emotions at bay. The crisp autumn air cooled his skin, but sweat trickled down his face and soaked the back of his shirt. His muscles ached with the relentless work, but the physical exhaustion was a welcome relief from the turmoil in his mind.

He had been taking on odd jobs around Millbrook for days—anything to keep his hands busy and his thoughts quiet. But no matter how hard he worked, no matter how many fences he repaired, or how many logs he split, the memories were always there, waiting for him in the quiet moments.

With the memories came the anger, simmering just beneath the surface and threatening to boil over. His jaw clenched as he swung the axe again, the wood splintering apart with a sharp crack. He paused for a moment, breathing hard, his chest tight with the weight of emotions he couldn't shake.

The image of Elizabeth flashed in his mind—her bright eyes, her innocent smile, the sound of her laughter echoing in the air. She had been so full of life, so carefree, her small hand slipping into his as they walked along the riverbank. But those memories were always fleeting, quickly overtaken by the darker ones. He could still hear her labored breathing, the shallow gasps as pneumonia had ravaged her young body. He could still see the fear in her eyes as she struggled to take each breath, her small frame shaking with the effort.

Nathan's chest tightened, the grief rising like a wave, threatening to pull him under. He had been helpless, watching his little girl slip away from him, powerless to stop it. He had prayed and begged for a miracle, but in the end, there had been nothing but silence. And then, after Elizabeth was gone, everything had fallen apart.

But it wasn't just Elizabeth's death that haunted him. It was what came after. The way he had failed Leslie—the woman he had promised to love and protect. After Elizabeth's death, Nathan had grown distant, retreating into himself, unable to face the reality of their loss. He had buried his pain deep, refusing to talk about it, refusing to let anyone in. And in doing so, he had left Leslie to carry her grief alone.

Nathan sat at the kitchen table, staring down at his cold cup of coffee. The house was unbearably quiet, every room filled with the absence of Elizabeth's laughter. It had been weeks since they had buried her, and yet the silence still felt new, raw, like a fresh wound that hadn't begun to heal.

He could hear the distant sound of Leslie moving around in the other room, her soft footsteps barely audible over the ticking of the clock on the wall. She had been busy cleaning, organizing, and doing anything she could to keep her hands moving.

Nathan knew she was hurting and needed him, but he didn't know how to help her. He didn't know how to help himself. So he had withdrawn, sinking into the numbness that had settled over him like a heavy blanket.

Leslie appeared in the doorway, her face pale, her eyes red from crying. She stood there for a moment, watching him, her expression a mixture of sorrow and frustration.

"Nathan," she said softly, her voice trembling. "We need to talk."

He didn't look up. "What is there to say?"

Leslie crossed the room, her steps slow and tentative, and sat across from him. She reached for his hand, her touch light as if she were afraid he might pull away. "We lost her," she said, her voice breaking. "We both lost her. But it feels like I'm losing you too."

Nathan's jaw tightened, guilt gnawing at him. He knew she was right. He had been shutting her out, retreating into his pain. But he didn't know how to fix it.

He didn't know how to talk about the things that haunted him. "I don't know what to say," he admitted, his voice barely above a whisper.

Leslie's grip on his hand tightened. "You don't have to say anything. Just… let me in. Let me help you."

Nathan pulled his hand away, the guilt twisting inside him. "I can't," he said, shaking his head. "I just… I can't."

Leslie's face crumpled, tears filling her eyes. She stood abruptly, wiping at her cheeks. "I can't do this alone, Nathan," she said, her voice tight with pain. "I need you. But I don't know how long I can hold on if you keep shutting me out."

She walked out of the kitchen, her footsteps heavy with the weight of her own grief, and Nathan had let her go. He had let her walk away without a word, too wrapped up in his own pain to reach out to her, to pull her back.

Back in Millbrook, Nathan opened his eyes, blinking against the memory. His hands trembled slightly as he wiped the sweat from his brow. No matter how much distance he tried to put between himself and his past, it always found a way to catch up with him. And with it came the bone-deep guilt that he had failed Leslie when she had needed him the most. He had let her carry her grief alone, and that failure had driven a wedge between them, one that could never be repaired.

He dropped the axe, the sound of it hitting the ground barely registering in his mind. His chest heaved with the weight of the emotions that had built up inside him, emotions he had buried for so long that they had begun to eat away at him from the inside.

The anger he had been carrying all these years wasn't just at God. It was at himself. He had pushed Leslie away and, in doing so, had lost her in more ways than one.

Across town, Lillian stood behind the counter at Thompson Supplies, staring at the open ledger in front of her. The numbers were bleak, and no matter how many times she went over them, they never seemed to add up. The shelves behind her were growing emptier by the day, and with winter fast approaching, the pressure to stock up on supplies was becoming more urgent. But the prices had risen sharply, and Lillian was already struggling to make ends meet.

She sighed, rubbing her temples as the weight of it all pressed down on her. It felt like she was constantly swimming against the tide, barely keeping her head above water. The store had been her lifeline after Henry's death, a way to provide for her children and keep herself busy, but lately, it felt like it was slipping through her fingers.

Outside, Samuel and Grace played in the dirt, their laughter a small comfort in the midst of the chaos. They were still so young, so full of life, and Lillian was determined to keep it that way. She didn't want them to know the full extent of their struggles; she didn't want them to carry the weight of the world on their small shoulders. But they were perceptive. They knew things weren't right, even if they didn't fully understand.

The door to the shop creaked open, and Mrs. Helen Granger stepped inside, her kind eyes crinkling in a smile as she held out a basket of eggs. "Thought you might be able to use these," she said, her voice gentle. "The hens have been busy, and we've got more than we need."

Lillian's throat tightened as she took the basket, gratitude swelling in her chest. "Thank you, Mrs. Granger," she said softly. "This means more than you know."

Mrs. Granger reached out and patted her arm. "We've all got to look out for each other, dear. Especially in times like these." Lillian nodded, her heart heavy with the knowledge that she wasn't the only one struggling.

The whole town felt the effects of the Great Depression, and everyone was doing their best to get by. But some days, it felt like she was barely holding it together, no matter how hard she tried.

Chapter Ten: The Weight of Silence

The following Sunday, the small wooden church in Millbrook was filled with the quiet murmur of families settling into their pews. The soft notes of the piano floated through the air as the congregation gathered, exchanging nods and hushed greetings. The familiar warmth of the church was a welcome respite from the outside world, a place where they could find comfort, even in the midst of uncertainty.

Nathan slipped through the back door, keeping his head down as he found a seat in the last pew. He didn't want to be noticed, didn't want to engage in conversation. He just wanted to sit in the back, unnoticed, and listen in silence. He wasn't sure why he had come. Maybe it was the pull of something familiar, or maybe it was Lillian's quiet encouragement that had brought him here.

"Today's scripture comes from Matthew 11:28-30," Reverend James began, his voice steady as he scanned the congregation. "'Come to me, all who labor and are heavy laden, and I will give you rest. Take my yoke upon you, and learn from me, for I am gentle and lowly in heart, and you will find rest for your souls. For my yoke is easy, and my burden is light.'"

Nathan sat rigid in the last pew, staring straight ahead but not really seeing anything. The reverend's words seemed to echo around him, reaching out, but he wasn't ready to let them in. Rest? How could there be rest when his heart had been torn apart? When his burdens were anything but light?

The memories of Elizabeth and Leslie clung to him like shadows, always lurking just behind him, constantly reminding him of what he had lost. Reverend James continued, his voice filled with compassion.

"We all carry burdens in this life. Some are visible—the struggles to put food on the table, keep a roof over our heads, and provide for our families. But some burdens are hidden deep inside us, heavy weights we carry alone. Grief, guilt, anger—these are the burdens that press hardest on our hearts. We try to carry them on our own, thinking we can bear the weight. But we aren't meant to carry them alone."

Nathan's fists clenched in his lap. The reverend's words felt too close to the truth—too personal as if the man knew exactly what Nathan had been carrying all these years. The guilt, the anger, the overwhelming grief that had become a part of him. He had tried to carry it all alone, convinced he had to. Convinced that no one else could understand the depth of his pain. Not even God.

"We're not meant to carry these burdens alone," Reverend James said again, his voice soft but firm. "The Lord is offering to share in our pain, to carry the weight that we cannot. But we have to be willing to let Him. We have to trust Him enough to lay our burdens at His feet."

Nathan's throat tightened. Trust? That was the hardest part. He had trusted once. He had prayed, begged for help, for relief from the crushing weight of his grief. But in the end, he had been left alone, burdened with the loss of his wife and daughter. The anger rose in him again, a familiar heat that made it hard to breathe. Reverend James stepped away from the pulpit, his gaze sweeping over the congregation.

"Some of you may be wondering where God is in your suffering. You may be asking, 'Why did He let this happen? Why didn't He stop it?' And those are questions we all wrestle with at some point. But the truth is that God never promised us a life without pain. He promised to walk with us through it. To carry us when we cannot carry ourselves."

Nathan's jaw tightened, his teeth grinding together. Walk with us? Carry us through the pain? Where had God been when Leslie had died in that car crash? Where had He been when Elizabeth had drawn her last breath, her small body unable to fight the pneumonia that had stolen her life?

Nathan had been left to carry that burden alone. No one had been there to help him—not even God.

The final hymn began, the soft notes of the piano filling the air as the congregation rose to their feet to sing. Nathan remained seated, staring at the floor, his heart pounding in his chest. When the song ended, and the others began to file out of the church, he slipped out the back door, unnoticed by the rest of the congregation. He couldn't stay in that place any longer. He needed air. He needed space.

Nathan's boots crunched against the gravel path as he made his way toward Willowbend River, the sound of the water growing louder as he neared the familiar clearing. The late afternoon sun filtered through the trees, casting long shadows over the ground, but Nathan barely noticed. His mind was spinning, the reverend's words echoing in his head, mixing with the memories that refused to leave him alone.

He reached the riverbank, the sound of the rushing water filling the quiet around him. The river had always been a place of refuge for him, its steady flow a reminder that life moved on, even when everything else felt stuck in place. But today, even the river couldn't calm the storm inside him.

Nathan stood at the edge of the water, staring down at the swirling current, his fists clenched at his sides. The anger he had been holding back during the service finally rose to the surface, breaking free like a dam that had been holding it back for too long.

"You weren't there," he muttered, his voice rough with emotion. He took a step closer to the water, his chest tight with the weight of his grief. "You weren't there when I needed you. You weren't there when Leslie needed you."

The wind rustled the trees, the only answer to his angry plea. Nathan dropped to his knees at the river's edge, his hands digging into the earth as tears blurred his vision. "You took them from me," he whispered, his voice breaking. "You took everything from me, and I don't understand why."

The sound of the river rushing over the rocks filled the silence, but it did nothing to ease the ache in his chest. Nathan's breath came in short, shallow bursts as he stared down at the water, the reflection of the sky and trees distorted by the ripples.

He had carried this anger and guilt for so long, convinced that he had to bear it alone. Convinced that no one could understand the depth of his pain. Not even God. For a long time, Nathan stayed there, kneeling by the river, his hands clenching the dirt beneath him. The sun dipped lower in the sky, casting a golden light over the water, but Nathan felt no warmth from it. He felt empty and drained, the anger that had once burned so fiercely inside him slowly fading, leaving behind only the hollow ache of grief.

As dusk settled in and the sky darkened, Nathan finally stood, his legs stiff from the hours spent kneeling. He stared at the river one last time, the soft rush of the water the only sound in the quiet evening. He still didn't have the answers he needed. He still didn't understand why everything had happened the way it had.

But for the first time in years, he felt something shift inside him—something small, faint, and real. Maybe, just maybe, he didn't have to carry this burden alone.

Chapter Eleven: Through the Rain

The rain fell in a steady drizzle, its sound tapping softly against the windows of Thompson Supplies. The gray clouds hung low over the town, casting everything in a muted, dreary light. Lillian stood behind the counter, staring out at the empty street, her hands absentmindedly wiping the same spot on the worn wooden countertop. The shelves behind her were growing more bare by the day, and no matter how hard she tried to make the numbers in her ledger work, they just wouldn't.

She had made the difficult decision to close the store three days a week, cutting her hours to save on expenses. It was a gamble—fewer hours meant fewer sales, but she couldn't keep the store open full-time with how little stock she had left. Every day felt like a battle, and the rain outside only magnified the weight pressing down on her chest.

Outside, the street was nearly deserted. People in town had grown used to staying indoors during the long, wet days of fall, doing their best to stretch what little food and money they had left.

The threat of rationing was becoming a reality as families whispered about the possibility of running out of essentials before winter fully set in. A flash of movement at the corner of her eye drew Lillian's attention. Samuel and Grace ran past the store, their shoes splashing in puddles as they chased after one another, their laughter momentarily breaking through the stillness.

For a brief moment, Lillian smiled, but the worry never fully left her. She had tried to shield her children from the worst of it, but they were growing up too fast. Samuel was starting to understand just how hard things were becoming.

With a deep sigh, Lillian turned the sign on the door to "Closed" and stepped outside, pulling her coat tighter around her as the rain continued to fall. She couldn't help but wonder how much longer she could keep the store open at all.

The rain pattered against Nathan's hat, running in rivulets down the brim as he walked through the muddy streets. He kept his head low. His hands shoved deep into his coat pockets as he walked toward the edge of town. The weight of his recent breakdown by the river still clung to him, the anger and guilt swirling in his chest like a storm he couldn't control.

He wasn't sure why he was leaving, but the thought of staying in Millbrook, of confronting his pain day after day, was too much to bear. His footsteps were heavy on the wet earth as he passed the rows of small houses, each one dark and quiet as the rain fell.

His plan was simple: walk out of town and keep walking until he didn't have to feel the weight of everything he had lost. But deep down, he knew running wouldn't change anything. As he neared the edge of town, a familiar voice stopped him in his tracks.

"Nathan."

He turned to see Reverend James standing under a nearby tree, his coat pulled tight around him to ward off the rain. The reverend's sharp eyes studied him long before he spoke again.

"You heading somewhere?"

Nathan looked away, his jaw tightening. "Just needed some air," he muttered.

Reverend James stepped closer, his boots sinking into the muddy ground. "Seems to me you were headed a little farther than just for air."

Nathan let out a slow breath, his shoulders sagging. "I don't know what I'm doing, Reverend."

The reverend didn't respond right away. Instead, he gestured toward a nearby bench, partially sheltered from the rain by the overhanging branches of an old oak tree. "Why don't we sit for a moment?"

For a second, Nathan hesitated, but something in the reverend's calm demeanor made him relent. He followed him to the bench, the cold rain still falling softly around them as they sat down.

Reverend James pulled a worn leather Bible from his coat pocket, turning it over in his hands as he looked at Nathan. "You've been carrying a heavy burden for a long time, son."

Nathan's throat tightened, the weight of the reverend's words hitting too close to home. "You don't know the half of it."

"I might know more than you think," the reverend said quietly. He opened the Bible and flipped to a well-worn page. "I've seen a lot of people come and go through this town, Nathan. Many folks are trying to outrun something, thinking they can leave their pain behind. But it never works, does it?"

Nathan stared at the ground, his jaw clenched. "No," he admitted, his voice rough. "It doesn't."

Reverend James nodded, as if he had expected the answer.

He glanced down at the Bible in his lap, his fingers tracing the lines of the page before he began to read aloud. "'Therefore, do not be anxious, saying, "What shall we eat?" or "What shall we drink?" or "What shall we wear?" For the Gentiles seek after all these things, and your heavenly Father knows that you need them all. But seek first the kingdom of God and his righteousness, and all these things will be added to you.'" (Matthew 6:31-33)

Nathan shifted uncomfortably, the familiar anger rising in his chest. "It's not that simple, Reverend."

"No," Reverend James agreed. "It's not simple. Faith rarely is."

He paused, closing the Bible gently. "But it's what we've got. And right now, people are holding on by the thinnest of threads in this town. You included."

Nathan's hands tightened into fists in his lap. "I've tried to have faith," he said, his voice low. "I tried to trust that everything would be okay. And look where it got me. I lost everything."

The reverend was silent for a long moment, the rain filling the space between them. Finally, he spoke, his voice quiet but firm. "You're not the only one who's lost something, Nathan. This town is full of people who've lost more than they ever thought they could bear. But they're still here. They're still fighting."

Nathan looked up, his eyes meeting the reverend's for the first time.

"I don't know how." Reverend James smiled faintly, though there was sadness in his eyes. "Neither do they. But they're doing it anyway."

The two men sat silently for a while, the rain continuing to fall around them. The quiet between them was heavy but not uncomfortable.

Finally, Reverend James spoke again, his voice thoughtful. "There's talk in town about rationing. Families are running low on food, and with winter coming, it's only going to get harder."

Nathan frowned. "What do you mean, rationing?" "We've got to make sure everyone gets enough to get by," the reverend explained. "We're talking about cutting back on portions, sharing what we have, making sure no one goes hungry. It's not official yet, but it's coming. People are scared."

Nathan's stomach tightened at the thought. He had seen what hunger could do to a town—to families. He had seen the way it tore people apart, the way desperation turned neighbors against each other.

"Do you think it'll be enough?" Nathan asked, his voice quieter now.

"I don't know," Reverend James admitted. "But we have to try. And I think we need you here to help."

Nathan's brow furrowed, surprised by the reverend's words. "Me?"

Reverend James looked at him steadily. "You've got more to offer than you think, Nathan. This town needs every hand it can get. People look up to you, even if you don't see it."

Nathan's chest tightened, the familiar mix of guilt and shame rising again. He had spent so long feeling like he was nothing but a burden like he had failed everyone he cared about. But maybe—just maybe—there was something he could do. Something that mattered. For the first time in a long time, Nathan felt the slightest flicker of hope.

Chapter Twelve: Ghosts of the Past

The evening light filtered through the trees, casting long shadows over the narrow river. Grace was sitting near the edge of the field, her small hands clutching a worn doll as she hummed quietly to herself. Lillian was inside the house, preparing a simple supper for her children, while Samuel worked to gather wood. It was the kind of peaceful, late autumn evening that might have seemed idyllic if it weren't for the weight of hardship hanging over them all.

Nathan stood at a distance, watching Grace as she played, the soft hum of her voice drifting on the breeze. She was so small, so innocent—unaware of the struggles the adults around her faced. But as he watched her, something shifted.

His heart twisted painfully, a cold shiver running down his spine as Grace's form seemed to blur at the edges, her small figure morphing into someone else—someone he hadn't seen in years. His breath hitched in his chest as Elizabeth appeared before him, sitting in the same spot Grace had just been, her delicate hands clutching her favorite doll. Her golden hair, pulled back in neat braids, caught the last rays of the setting sun, and her smile—oh, her smile—was as radiant as it had always been.

Nathan froze, his heart pounding in his ears. "Elizabeth?" His voice was barely more than a whisper, his legs rooted to the ground. It was impossible. She had been gone for so long, but there she was, sitting right there in front of him as if the years had never passed. She looked up at him, her eyes—those same deep blue eyes—wide and innocent.

"Daddy, will you come play with me?"

His knees felt weak, and the world seemed to tilt around him. He took a hesitant step forward, his mind racing, unable to comprehend what was happening. But just as suddenly as the vision had appeared, it began to slip away. The small figure blurred, shifting back into Grace, who was still humming quietly, unaware of Nathan's turmoil. He blinked rapidly, his heart still racing. Clarity returned, the weight of reality crashing back down on him like a blow to the chest.

Grace turned to look at him, her expression innocent and unknowing, and the sight only deepened the ache in his chest. Nathan stumbled backward, his breath coming in shallow gasps. He couldn't stay here. He couldn't let them see the cracks in his mind—couldn't let them see how broken he really was. Without a word, he turned on his heel and hurried toward the river, his footsteps uneven as he fled.

The rushing sound of Willowbend River filled the air as Nathan reached the water's edge. The familiar sight of the river should have calmed him, but instead, his chest felt tight, the panic rising in his throat. His hands trembled as he ran them through his hair, gripping at the strands as if trying to ground himself in the present, but the memories—no, the visions—kept pulling him back.

He stumbled to his knees by the bank. He didn't trust himself anymore. He didn't trust his mind. But what he saw next made his breath catch in his throat.

Leslie.

She stood at the edge of the river, her form bathed in the soft light of the setting sun, her hair cascading over her shoulders like it had all those years ago. She looked exactly as she had before everything had fallen apart—before Elizabeth had died, before the crash, before the world had taken everything from them.

"Leslie…" Nathan's voice cracked as he spoke her name, his hands gripping the earth beneath him.

She was so beautiful—so real. He could almost reach out and touch her. But she didn't speak. She stood there, her eyes filled with sadness, her lips slightly parted as if she were about to say something, but no words came. Nathan's heart pounded in his chest as he stared at her, his breath coming in shallow gasps. Was she real? Or was he losing his mind entirely?

The sound of the river rushed in his ears, but it was drowned out by the flood of memories—the flood of what had happened the day the stock market had crashed.

The noise had been overwhelming, like a wave crashing over him that he couldn't escape. The news had spread through the streets like wildfire, panic rising in the air as men and women shouted, their faces pale with fear. The stock market had collapsed, taking with it every ounce of security Nathan had worked so hard to build. His business, his savings—everything was gone in an instant, wiped out in a crash that he hadn't seen coming. Nathan had stood in the crowded street, his heart pounding as he tried to make sense of the chaos around him.

Men were running toward the bank, desperate to withdraw whatever was left of their savings, but the doors had already been shut, and the windows boarded up. People were screaming and crying, the weight of their losses too much to bear.

Leslie had been home with Elizabeth, completely unaware of the storm brewing. Nathan had walked back to their small house in a daze, the reality of what had happened sinking in with every step he took. His hands had trembled as he opened the door, the weight of his failure crashing down on him like a tidal wave.

"Leslie," he had whispered, his voice barely audible as he entered the house.

She looked up from the kitchen table, smiling as she tended to Elizabeth, who had been playing with her dolls on the floor. "What is it?" she had asked, her brow furrowing with concern.

But Nathan couldn't find the words to explain. He had collapsed into a chair, his head in his hands as the enormity of their situation settled in.

"We've lost everything," he had finally whispered, his voice breaking. "It's all gone."

Nathan's chest heaved as the memories flooded his mind, his vision blurring as he stared at the river. The weight of it all was too much. The guilt, the shame, the anger—it was crushing him. He had failed them. He had failed Leslie, and he had failed Elizabeth. He closed his eyes, his hands shaking as he gripped the earth beneath him.

"I'm sorry," he whispered, his voice hoarse with emotion. "I'm so sorry." The sound of footsteps behind him made him stiffen, but he didn't turn around. He didn't want anyone to see him like this—broken and lost.

"Nathan." The voice was soft and gentle. He recognized it immediately. Lillian. He slowly turned, his eyes filled with unshed tears as he met her gaze. She stood a few feet away, her auburn hair damp from the rain, her blue eyes filled with concern. She didn't say anything else—she didn't need to. The understanding in her expression was enough.

Nathan looked away, his hands still trembling. "I'm losing my mind, Lillian," he admitted, his voice barely above a whisper. "I don't know what's real anymore."

Lillian stepped closer, her footsteps soft on the wet earth. She knelt beside him, her hand gently resting on his arm. "You're not losing your mind," she said softly. "You've just been carrying too much for too long."

Nathan's chest tightened at her words. He had been carrying it all—alone—for far too long. They sat in the misting rain, the river rushing by them, the weight of their unspoken words hanging in the air. It wasn't a solution. It wasn't a fix. But it was a start.

Chapter Thirteen: A Cold Light of Hope

A week later, the wind howled through the narrow streets of Millbrook, its icy fingers creeping into every crevice, pulling at the edges of coats and scarves. The first cold weather had arrived, its presence unmistakable, biting at the skin and turning breaths into vapor clouds.

The small town, already quiet from the weight of the Great Depression, seemed even more subdued under the leaden sky. Smoke curled lazily from chimneys, but it did little to chase away the deep chill that settled into homes and hearts alike. Nathan pulled his coat tighter as he stood by the river, the stillness of the narrow waters a stark contrast to the storm of emotions inside him. The cold seemed fitting, a physical manifestation of the ice that had gripped his soul since losing his family.

He'd spent the better part of the afternoon avoiding town, keeping to the outskirts where he could breathe without the weight of expectation or conversation. The town was preparing for the Thanksgiving church service that evening, but the idea of sitting through a sermon on gratitude felt like too much. How could he be thankful when everything he had loved was gone? The cold wind whipped around him, and Nathan closed his eyes, trying to block out the painful memories that surfaced unbidden.

The wooden church was nearly full when Nathan arrived, slipping in through the back as he always did. His boots left damp footprints on the floor, the cold from outside following him in like an unwelcome guest. The dim light from the candles flickered against the walls, casting long shadows that danced across the pews. Despite the warmth of the bodies huddled together, the chill still lingered in the air, a reminder that the winter had arrived in full force.

Lillian sat near the front, her children beside her, their faces glowing in the candlelight. Nathan's gaze briefly lingered on her before he looked away, finding his usual seat at the back. He kept his head down, not wanting to meet the eyes of anyone who might offer a nod of recognition. He wasn't here to be seen—he was here to listen, though he wasn't sure why. The soft notes of the piano filled the air, the hymn familiar but tinged with a new melancholy.

The townspeople sang quietly, their voices low, as if the cold had sapped the energy from their bones. Grace fidgeted in her seat beside her mother, her wide eyes filled with curiosity and confusion. Nathan couldn't help but notice how small she looked, bundled up in her coat, her feet barely touching the ground.

After the hymn, Reverend James stepped forward, his worn Bible in hand. The man's face was lined with years of hardship, but his eyes still held that same quiet determination, the kind of faith that had weathered every storm life had thrown at him.

"Tonight," Reverend James began, his voice steady, "we gather to give thanks, even when it feels like there's little to be thankful for."

Nathan shifted in his seat, the familiar tightness in his chest returning. He stared at the floor, trying to tune out the words that felt like they were directed straight at him.

"We've all faced loss this year," Reverend James continued, his gaze sweeping over the congregation. "We've all known hunger, fear, and uncertainty. Many of you are worried about the long winter ahead, wondering if there will be enough to get by. But in the midst of all this, we are called to give thanks. Not because our lives are easy but because we have each other. We have our faith. And we hope that, no matter how dark it seems now, there is light ahead."

Nathan's hands clenched into fists on his lap. Hope. Faith. He'd had those once. He'd believed that things would get better, that God would carry him through the worst of it. But where had that faith been when he'd lost Leslie? Where had it been when Elizabeth had drawn her last breath? His heart ached with the weight of those questions, and the cold seemed to seep deeper into his bones.

The quiet voice of a child broke the stillness. Grace's small face turned up to her mother, and she tugged at Lillian's sleeve. "Mama," she whispered, her voice carrying in the silence, "why don't we have a big feast like in the stories?"

Lillian's smile was sad as she bent down to whisper back. "Because this year is different, Grace. But we're still thankful for what we have."

Grace's brow furrowed, her young mind unable to understand why everything had changed. She looked around the church, at the faces of the townspeople who sat with somber expressions, and then back at her mother. "But we don't have much."

Lillian squeezed her daughter's hand gently, her voice soft but firm. "We have each other. And that's what matters most."

Nathan watched the exchange, his chest tightening at the innocence of Grace's question. He had no answers for her, no explanations for why life had taken so much from them all. The sight of Lillian, so calm and steady in the face of everything, stirred something deep inside him. She was holding on, somehow, and it made him wonder if maybe—just maybe—he could too.

Reverend James closed his Bible, his eyes scanning the faces of his congregation. "We are all struggling. Some of us have lost work, others have lost loved ones. We are cold, we are hungry, and we are uncertain about what tomorrow will bring. But tonight, we remember that we are not alone. We lean on one another, find strength in our faith, and give thanks for the small blessings that remain."

The silence in the church was thick, the weight of the townspeople's collective grief and fear palpable. Many had lost their jobs when the mines closed, others had seen their crops fail, and more than a few families were facing the very real possibility of not making it through the winter without rationing what little food they had left.

Nathan looked around the room at the faces of people he had known for years. Some of them had grown thin from hunger, others had the hard, drawn look of those who had spent too many sleepless nights worrying about the future. He had been so focused on his own pain, his own loss, that he hadn't allowed himself to see just how much everyone else was suffering, too.

For the first time in what felt like forever, Nathan felt a flicker of something inside him—a small, fragile sense of connection to the people around him. Maybe Reverend James was right. Maybe, even in the midst of all this darkness, there was light ahead.

As the final hymn began, Nathan listened more closely than before. The song's words, about hope and faith and holding on through the storm, seemed to resonate in a way they hadn't before. He wasn't sure he believed in that hope yet, but he was starting to think that maybe he wanted to. The service ended with a soft murmur of voices as the townspeople slowly stood, bundling their coats tightly against the cold as they prepared to step back out into the freezing night. The warmth of the church lingered in the air, though, a small comfort in the face of the long winter ahead.

As Nathan stepped outside, the wind hit him with its familiar sharpness, but it didn't feel quite as unbearable as it had before. There was still a long road ahead, and he wasn't sure where it would lead. But he didn't feel completely alone for the first time in a long while.

Chapter Fourteen: A Town of Edge

The chill in the air seemed to seep into every corner of Millbrook, the once mild autumn giving way to the sharp bite of approaching winter. Frost rimmed the edges of the fields, and the gray sky hung heavy, pressing down on the small town. Though it was not yet fully winter, the cold had already begun to settle into the bones of the people.

The town felt tense, like a string pulled too tight, ready to snap. Earl Wilson, the town's blacksmith, stood by the forge in his shop, his breath visible in the frigid air as he hammered down on a glowing piece of metal. The heat from the fire was welcome, but even in the shop, the cold still nipped at his fingers. The rhythmic clang of his hammer filled the quiet space, offering a steady contrast to the unsettling quiet that had fallen over the town.

As Earl worked, Nathan arrived, stepping into the warmth of the shop. He hadn't been sure why he'd come, but something about the constant clanging of the blacksmith's hammer drew him in, offering a momentary reprieve from his racing thoughts.

"Morning," Earl grunted, barely looking up from his work.

He was a man of few words, preferring the company of his tools to that of people, but he'd always had a quiet respect for Nathan. He could sense the storm brewing in him, even if Nathan never spoke of it.

"Morning," Nathan replied, his voice rough from the cold. He lingered by the entrance, feeling the forge's heat on his face, but the chill in his bones remained. He watched Earl work for a moment, the clang of the hammer reverberating through the small shop.

After a long pause, Earl finally spoke again, his voice low and gruff. "Something on your mind, Grant?"

Nathan hesitated, unsure how to answer. The truth was, everything was on his mind—the memories of Elizabeth and Leslie, the growing tension in the town, the gnawing feeling that he didn't belong here or anywhere. But instead of unloading it all, he shook his head. "Just passing through."

Earl didn't press, but there was a flicker of understanding in his eyes as he glanced up from his work. "We're all passin' through, one way or another," he said, his voice carrying the weight of years spent watching people come and go. "But you don't always have to be movin' to find your way."

The words lingered in the air, heavy with meaning, but Nathan couldn't bring himself to respond. He offered a quiet nod of thanks before turning to leave, the sound of the hammer fading behind him as he stepped back out into the cold.

By the time Nathan returned to Riverside Boarding House, the afternoon light was already fading, casting long shadows over the narrow streets. The cold had only deepened, and the wind bit at his face as he pulled his coat tighter around him. The small town felt eerily quiet, as though everyone was holding their breath, waiting for something to happen.

Inside the boarding house, Mrs. Granger bustled about, tidying up the common area and checking on the few remaining boarders. Her sharp eyes darted to Nathan as he entered, but her expression softened when she saw him.

"Back already?" she asked, her voice as brisk as the wind outside, though there was a hint of warmth behind it.

Mrs. Granger had a reputation for being strict, but there was no denying that she cared deeply for the people under her roof. Nathan offered a faint smile, though it didn't reach his eyes. "Earl's shop was a little too warm for me today."

Mrs. Granger snorted, her hands busy wiping down a dusty countertop. "Warmth in this weather's a rare blessing. You ought to take it where you can find it."

Nathan didn't respond, his mind too preoccupied to make small talk. Instead, his gaze drifted to the window, where the trees swayed in the cold wind. He could feel the tension in the air—people were on edge, the cold making everything feel more precarious, more fragile.

Mrs. Granger seemed to sense the weight of his thoughts, and her no-nonsense demeanor softened for a moment. "The town's seen hard times before," she said quietly, her voice reassuring. "We've made it through worse winters than this. Folks'll get through it. You'll get through it."

Nathan wanted to believe her, but the knot in his chest wouldn't loosen. He offered a quiet nod before heading upstairs, where the cold draft from the windows made the small room feel even smaller.

Later that day, Nathan found himself crossing paths with Ryan, the young man who helped with odd jobs around town. Ryan had a bright, youthful energy that sometimes grated on Nathan, but there was something admirable in the boy's resilience: his determination to make the best of a bad situation.

"You headed out again?" Ryan asked, his breath coming out in visible puffs of air as he hefted a sack of supplies over his shoulder. "Thought you'd stick around the boarding house today."

Nathan shrugged. "Needed some air."

Ryan nodded, his expression thoughtful. "I get it. Sometimes it feels like this place is too small, you know? Like you gotta keep moving, or you'll get stuck."

Nathan glanced at him, surprised by the comment. "You ever think about leaving?"

Ryan laughed, though there was no real humor in it. "All the time. But where would I go? Everywhere's about the same these days." He paused, his gaze shifting to the horizon. "I figure I'll stay as long as I've got work. Ain't much else to do."

Nathan didn't reply, but Ryan's words struck a chord. He'd been running for so long, convinced that the next town would be better, that somewhere out there was where he could forget everything. But he was beginning to realize that no matter how far he went, the weight of his past would always follow him.

As the afternoon stretched into evening, the tension in the town seemed to thicken. People whispered about food shortages, the possibility of rationing, and the fear of a brutal winter looming over them like a dark cloud. Lillian struggled to keep Thompson Supplies running, but the stock was running low, and the cold had driven away most of her customers. Nathan passed the store on his way back from the blacksmith's, noticing Lillian talking quietly with a supplier. Her voice was low, her frustration barely concealed.

Nathan could see the strain in her posture, the way her shoulders sagged under the weight of the responsibility she carried. He wanted to help—wanted to do something—but he didn't know how. Instead, he kept walking, the cold wind biting at his face as he headed for the one place where he could think clearly.

The river was quiet when Nathan arrived, the water moving slowly under a thin layer of ice that had formed along the edges. The air was colder here, the trees bare and brittle against the darkening sky. Nathan stood at the edge, staring at the water, his breath coming in shallow bursts as his mind raced.

It wasn't long before the familiar feeling of dread settled over him, the memories creeping in like an unwelcome guest. He closed his eyes, his hands shaking as he tried to push them away, but it was useless. Suddenly, he saw her—Leslie, standing at the river's edge, her figure bathed in the soft, fading light of the evening. She was just as beautiful as he remembered, her hair flowing gently in the wind, her face a perfect picture of the past he had lost.

But there was sadness in her eyes, a deep, unspoken sorrow that cut through him like a knife. "Leslie…" Nathan whispered, his voice breaking as he reached out toward the vision. But she didn't move. She didn't speak. She just stood there, watching him with those eyes full of pain, and the weight of his guilt crushed him all over again. Nathan stumbled backward, falling to his knees in the cold, damp earth. "I'm sorry," he whispered, his voice hoarse with emotion. "I'm so sorry."

The footsteps behind him barely registered as he knelt by the river, lost in the swirling memories of his past. But when a gentle hand rested on his shoulder, he looked up, startled. Lillian, her auburn hair tousled by the wind, her blue eyes filled with concern. She didn't say anything at first—just knelt beside him, her presence steady and calm. "You're carrying too much."

For the first time in a long while, Nathan didn't have a reply. He just sat there, the weight of his past heavy on his shoulders, but Lillian's hand on his arm reminded him that maybe, just maybe, he didn't have to carry it alone.

Chapter Fifteen: Reaching for Hope

The morning was colder than it had been the day before, the sharp bite of frost hanging in the air as Nathan walked through the quiet streets of Millbrook. He had woken before dawn, the weight of his restless thoughts dragging him from sleep.

The vision of Leslie at the river still haunted him. Her sorrowful face burned into his memory like a scar. No matter how hard he tried, he couldn't shake the guilt, the feeling that he had failed her—and Elizabeth—in ways he could never fix.

He wandered through the town, the frost-covered ground crunching under his boots, his breath visible in the cold morning air. The streets were empty, the town still asleep, and for a moment, the quiet was a relief. It was easier to think here, away from the noise of his mind.

His walk took him to the church, where he had been helping with repairs.

Although small and worn with age, the church building was a place of quiet comfort. The rest of the repairs were simple—fixing broken hinges on the doors—but they gave him a sense of purpose, however small. It kept his hands busy and his mind occupied, even for a little while.

At Thompson Supplies, Lillian stood behind the counter, her eyes on the open ledger. The numbers, as always, didn't add up. No matter how many times she tried, there wasn't enough money. The reduced hours and the cold weather had kept customers away, and it was becoming harder to keep the store afloat. She rubbed her temples, trying to push away the ache of worry that had settled there.

Behind her, Grace and Samuel were sitting on the floor by the counter, playing quietly with a couple of old toys. Grace had her worn doll, and Samuel was busy stacking wooden blocks, his face serious as he concentrated on building the tallest tower he could manage. He had always been the more serious of the two, even at his young age, already taking on the weight of responsibilities he didn't fully understand.

Lillian glanced at them, her heart aching with love and worry. She had tried so hard to shield them from the worst of their struggles, but it was getting harder to hide the truth. How much longer could she keep this up?

"Mama?" Grace's voice pulled her from her thoughts. The little girl stood up, clutching her doll, her blue eyes wide with concern. "When are we gonna get more food?"

Lillian's chest tightened at the question. She had known this moment was coming, but hearing it from Grace's lips made the reality of their situation feel even heavier.

She knelt, brushing a strand of hair from Grace's forehead and forcing a smile. "Soon, sweetheart," she said softly. "We'll be alright."

Samuel looked up from his blocks, his face thoughtful. "But we're almost out, aren't we?" he asked quietly, his young voice filled with a seriousness that broke Lillian's heart.

She nodded, not trusting herself to speak for a moment. "We have enough for now," she said, her voice gentle but firm. "That's all that matters. Don't you worry about anything else."

Samuel nodded, but the look in his eyes told her he wasn't convinced. He was too smart for his age, too aware of the world around him. Lillian stood and watched as the two children returned to their toys, the weight of her responsibilities pressing down on her like a stone. How much longer could she pretend everything was fine?

Later that day, as Nathan worked at the church, the familiar sound of the hammer rang through the cold air. The repairs were simple, and for a few hours, he managed to push aside the thoughts that had been plaguing him. His hands worked automatically, fixing the door that started sagging on its hinges. It was enough to keep his mind occupied and quiet the storm inside him, at least for a little while. But the quiet didn't last.

As he worked, a commotion from down the street caught his attention. Voices—raised and urgent—echoed through the town square. Nathan paused, frowning as he recognized the sound of Earl Wilson's deep voice calling for help.

His gut twisted with sudden worry, and without thinking, he dropped the hammer and ran toward the sound. When he reached the blacksmith's shop, the scene that greeted him was chaotic.

Ryan, the young man who helped Earl, was sitting on the ground, his face twisted in pain, his hand wrapped in a rough cloth that was quickly turning dark with blood. Earl knelt beside him, his weathered face filled with concern, his hands steady as he tried to stop the bleeding.

"He got burned," Earl said gruffly as Nathan approached. "Wasn't watching close enough—iron was too hot. We need to get him looked at."

Nathan's chest tightened at the sight of Ryan's injury. The burn looked terrible, and the cloth did not help. Without a word, Nathan crouched beside Ryan, his gaze sharp as he assessed the damage. The young man was sweating, his face pale, his breathing shallow.

"We need to get him to Mrs. Granger. She'll know what to do." Earl nodded, his hands steady as he carefully helped Ryan to his feet.

"She's better with this sort of thing than I am." They made their way to Riverside Boarding House, where Mrs. Granger met them at the door, her sharp eyes immediately assessing the situation. Without a word, she ushered them inside, her no-nonsense demeanor taking charge as she led them to a small room where Ryan could lie down. Her hands were steady. Her movements were precise as she tended to the burn, applying a salve and wrapping it in fresh bandages. "Foolish boy," she muttered under her breath, though her tone was more concerned than scolding. "You'll be fine, but you'll need to rest that hand for a while."

Ryan winced but nodded, his face pale with pain. "Thanks, Mrs. Granger." Nathan stood nearby, watching in silence as Mrs. Granger worked. He hadn't known the older woman well, but he had heard enough about her to know that she was the one people turned to when something like this happened. Her hands were steady, her face calm, and Nathan felt a strange sense of peace settle over him for a moment. Maybe there was something to be said for staying in one place—something to be said for people like Mrs. Granger and Earl, who didn't run.

As the day ended, Lillian sat at the small desk in the back room of Thompson Supplies, the ledger and bills spread out before her. The numbers didn't matter anymore—they were all the same. The truth was inescapable, and as much as she tried to pretend otherwise, she couldn't keep the store open much longer if things didn't change.

Her thoughts drifted to Henry, as they often did when everything felt too heavy to carry. She missed him—missed his steady presence, his quiet strength. His death had left a hole in her heart that nothing could fill, and every day since, it had been a battle to keep going, to keep providing for Grace and Samuel.

She reached for the Bible that sat beside the ledger, opening it to a familiar passage: Isaiah 40:31, "But those who hope in the Lord will renew their strength. They will soar on wings like eagles; they will run and not grow weary, they will walk and not be faint."

The words had always brought her comfort, but today they felt heavy, like a promise she wasn't sure she could believe. She closed the Bible, resting her head in her hands as she prayed softly, asking for the strength to keep going, to face the days ahead, to hold on just a little longer.

Chapter Sixteen: Pieces of a Broken World

The wind had picked up overnight, sweeping through Millbrook with a biting chill that seemed to cut through everything in its path. Nathan stood outside the church, his breath coming in short, visible puffs, his hands tucked deep into his coat pockets to ward off the cold.

The old building loomed in front of him, its weathered walls a reminder of time and endurance. He found some strange comfort in that—how the church had stood for years, weathering the elements and the struggles of those who sought solace within its walls.

He adjusted the weight of the plank on his shoulder, and the ache in his arms was a welcome distraction from the weight of his thoughts. His muscles burned with the effort of carrying the wood, but he didn't mind. It gave him something to focus on—other than the memories that haunted him, memories of Leslie and Elizabeth, memories of all the ways he had failed them.

The repairs on the church were slow, the cold making the work harder than it should have been, but Nathan preferred it that way. It meant he could lose himself in the rhythm of the hammer, the steady pounding of nails into wood. He'd been working on patching the roof, fixing broken beams, and mending the door that sagged on its hinges. The work was simple, but it was enough to keep his hands busy and quiet the storm inside his head—if only for a little while.

As he reached for another nail, his gaze fell on the Bible that sat on the nearby bench, left behind by one of the churchgoers. It had been there for days, its worn leather cover cracked with age, the edges of the pages frayed from years of use. Nathan paused, his hand hovering over the hammer as something pulled at him, something quiet and insistent.

Without thinking, he set the hammer down and reached for the book, his fingers brushing over the weathered surface. He hadn't touched a Bible in years, not since the world had fallen apart around him, but now, with the cold wind biting at his skin and the quiet of the churchyard settling over him, he felt a strange pull.

He flipped the book open, the pages rustling softly in the wind, and his eyes landed on a verse that seemed to leap off the page: Isaiah 43:2 – "When you pass through the waters, I will be with you; and when you pass through the rivers, they will not sweep over you. When you walk through the fire, you will not be burned; the flames will not set you ablaze."

The words hit him hard, settling in his chest with a weight he hadn't expected. I will be with you. He hadn't thought about God in a long time. Not since the days when he'd stood by Elizabeth's bedside, praying for a miracle that never came. Not since he'd buried his wife and child, not since the guilt and grief had swallowed him whole. But now, standing there with the Bible open in his hands, he felt something stir inside him—a flicker of something he couldn't quite name.

The wind picked up, snapping him out of his thoughts, and he quickly closed the Bible, setting it back on the bench. The verse stayed with him like an echo in his mind. When you walk through the fire, you will not be burned. It felt like a promise, one he wasn't sure he deserved, but maybe—just maybe—something was waiting for him if he could find the strength to stop running.

At Riverside Boarding House, Mrs. Granger moved swiftly through the small kitchen, her sharp eyes darting between the stove and the young woman seated at the table. Rachel Parker, a young woman in her 20s with dark hair and eyes, was the new guest who had arrived that morning. She sat with her hands wrapped tightly around a cup of tea, her face pale and drawn from the cold. Rachel's eyes were hollow, dark circles beneath them, and her once fine clothes were now frayed and worn at the edges.

Mrs. Granger had seen her kind before. People who had been running for so long forgot what it felt like to stand still. She didn't pry, didn't ask questions, but she could see the weight of the girl's journey in every line of her face.

"You'll need more than tea to warm you up," Mrs. Granger said, her voice brisk as she placed a plate of bread and cheese in front of Rachel. "Eat up. You look like you haven't had a proper meal in weeks."

Rachel's hands trembled as she reached for the bread, her fingers thin and pale. "Thank you," she whispered, her voice barely audible. She glanced up, her eyes meeting Mrs. Granger's for a brief moment before dropping back down to her cup. "I... I don't know how to repay you."

Mrs. Granger waved a hand dismissively, pulling out a chair and sitting across from her. "You're not here to repay anyone. You're here to rest and eat, and that's all you need to worry about for now."

Rachel nodded slowly, though the tension in her shoulders didn't ease. She stared down at the plate in front of her, the smell of the bread making her stomach growl, though she wasn't sure if she could eat.

The weight of her journey pressed down on her, the memory of her husband and the life she had left behind still fresh in her mind. "I left him," she said quietly, not looking up. Her voice was flat, almost mechanical as if she were reciting something she had practiced. "I couldn't stay. I couldn't... I couldn't do it anymore."

Mrs. Granger watched her carefully, her expression softening just slightly. "A lot of folks leave things behind they don't want to. You did what you had to."

Rachel swallowed hard, her throat tight with unshed tears. She had been running for weeks, hopping from town to town, never staying long enough for anyone to ask questions. But here, in this small town with its quiet streets and people who seemed to care without asking anything in return, she felt a strange sense of... safety. It was something she hadn't felt in a long time.

"I didn't mean to stay," Rachel added, her voice trembling. "I just needed to rest. I'll be gone in the morning."

Mrs. Granger raised an eyebrow, her lips twitching in a faint smile. "We'll see about that."

Over at the blacksmith's shop, Earl was back at the forge, his hands steady as he shaped metal over the flames. The rhythmic sound of the hammer rang through the air, a familiar melody in the cold morning. Despite the bandage on his hand, Ryan was working beside him, his face set in concentration. The burn had slowed him down, but he couldn't sit still for long, and Earl had given up trying to get him to rest.

"You're a stubborn one," Earl muttered as he watched Ryan attempt to lift a heavy piece of metal. "You're gonna end up burnin' yourself again if you're not careful."

Ryan grinned, though the effort sent a sharp jolt of pain through his bandaged hand. "Can't sit still, Earl. You know that."

Earl shook his head, though there was a hint of fondness in his gruff tone. "You keep that up, and you'll be no good to me for a while."

He stepped closer, taking the metal from Ryan's hands. "Go easy, boy. You'll be useless to anyone if you push too hard."

Ryan nodded, though he didn't slow down.

Back at Thompson Supplies, Lillian stood at the counter, her gaze drifting to the window as the townspeople passed by, their faces drawn and lined with worry. The cold had deepened, and with it, the strain of surviving through the long months ahead. The store was quiet, the shelves half-empty, and Lillian knew that no matter how hard she tried to stretch the supplies, it wouldn't be enough to last through the winter.

She sighed, her fingers tracing the edge of the worn counter. The weight of everything seemed heavier lately—the store, the children, the endless struggle to keep going. She wasn't sure how much longer she could hold it all together, but somehow, she did. Somehow, every morning, she got up and did what needed to be done.

The door chimed, and Lillian looked up to see Nathan standing in the doorway, his coat dusted with frost, his dark hair damp from the cold. He gave her a small nod as he stepped inside, his eyes lingering on her for a moment before he spoke.

"Roof's done," he said, his voice low. "Should hold through the winter." Lillian smiled, though the weight of her worries still pressed down on her.

"Thank you," she said quietly. "I don't know what I'd do without your help."

Nathan shrugged, his gaze softening just a little. "Just doing what I can." Lillian watched him for a moment longer, feeling the faintest flicker of warmth amid the cold. It wasn't just the help he gave with the store, or the repairs around town—it was something deeper, something quieter. Nathan didn't speak much, didn't ask for thanks, but his presence had become a steady, comforting part of her days. Even though they both carried their own burdens, there was a silent understanding between them, a shared struggle that neither had to explain.

"I appreciate it," Lillian added softly, her voice barely rising above the wind that rattled the door behind him. "You've done more than you know."

Nathan looked down, his hands shoved deep into his coat pockets. "Just trying to keep busy," he muttered, though there was a weight to his words that Lillian didn't miss.

She nodded, recognizing the heaviness that lingered between them. There were things he didn't say—things he carried with him just as she carried her own grief and worries. But she didn't press him, didn't ask for more than he was willing to give. In this town, people knew how to respect the silences between them.

"Samuel and Grace have been talking about you," she said after a pause, her lips curving into a small smile. "They're convinced you're some kind of hero, fixing the roof and helping at the church."

Nathan's expression softened slightly, though a shadow still flickered in his eyes. "They're good kids. Strong."

Lillian's smile faded as she thought of her children—how they had been forced to grow up too fast, how they had learned to carry the weight of a world that wasn't kind. "They have to be," she replied quietly. "But they've been better since you've been around."

Nathan didn't respond, but the look in his eyes told her that he understood. They stood in silence for a moment, the unspoken words between them hanging in the cold air. Lillian wished, for a fleeting moment, that things were different—that life hadn't been so hard, that the weight of their losses didn't pull at them so much. But this was the world they lived in, and all they could do was keep going.

After a long pause, Nathan finally shifted, pulling his coat tighter around him. "I'll stop by again tomorrow," he said gruffly, stepping toward the door. "See if there's anything else that needs fixing."

Lillian nodded, watching as he left, the cold wind rushing in behind him. She stood at the counter for a while after he'd gone, her thoughts heavy but her heart just a little lighter.

There was something about Nathan, something about the way he showed up even when he didn't have to, that made her feel like maybe—just maybe—they could get through this. Together, even if in silence.

Outside, the wind had grown colder, sweeping through the empty streets of Millbrook with a force that carried the weight of the season. The town felt quieter now, more withdrawn, as winter approached and the hardships deepened. But amidst the cold and the struggle, there was still life—there were still people holding on, still helping one another in the ways they could.

At the blacksmith shop, Earl glanced up at the darkening sky, his weathered face creased with concern. "Storm's coming," he muttered to himself as he doused the flames of the forge for the evening. "Gonna be a rough one."

Ryan stood nearby, his hand still bandaged but his spirits undeterred. "We'll make it through," he said with a small grin, though the tension in his voice betrayed the worry he carried.

"Always do." Earl shot him a look but didn't argue.

"Get yourself home before it gets any worse," he said, his tone gruff but laced with care. "Mrs. Granger's probably got her eye on you already."

Ryan chuckled, though it was short-lived. He turned, heading for the boarding house, the cold biting at his skin as he walked. He thought of Rachel, the new woman who had arrived that morning, and wondered if she'd stay. Millbrook had a way of pulling people in, even when they didn't plan on staying.

At Riverside Boarding House, Rachel sat by the fire in the small parlor, her hands wrapped around a cup of tea that had long since gone cold. She stared into the flames, her thoughts drifting back to the life she had left behind—the husband she had fled, the home that had never really felt like home.

Mrs. Granger bustled in from the kitchen, her sharp eyes taking in the scene with a quick glance. "Storm's coming," she said as she added another log to the fire. "You best settle in. No one's going anywhere tonight."

Rachel nodded, though her thoughts were far away. She wasn't sure if she could stay—not in Millbrook or anywhere. But something about the town, about how people had taken her in without question, made her wonder if maybe… just maybe… she could stop running for now.

Mrs. Granger sat beside her, her hands busy with knitting. She didn't say anything, but her presence was enough—a steady reminder that people took care of their own in this small town.

And Rachel felt a flicker of something almost like hope for the first time in a long time.

Chapter Seventeen: The Cold Sets In

The last of the wood creaked under Nathan's hands as he secured it on the church roof. His fingers were numb from the cold, his breath visible in short puffs as he worked. The repairs had taken longer than expected, and now, with winter bearing down on Millbrook, they were running out of materials. The church was a symbol of hope for many in the town, but it was falling apart just like everything else seemed to be.

Below, on the ground, Reverend James watched Nathan's progress, his face pulled tight in concentration.

The reverend had been trying to stay optimistic, but even his words of encouragement had grown weary with the passing days. "You've done a fine job, Nathan," he called up, his voice edged with something that sounded less like hope and more like determination. "We'll be alright."

Nathan didn't respond right away. His hands worked mechanically, tightening the last nail before he finally spoke. "It'll hold," he said simply, though the exhaustion in his voice was impossible to hide.

Reverend James nodded, his breath fogging in the cold air as he stepped back to survey the work. "It has to," he murmured to himself, though Nathan heard him.

They were both thinking the same thing—no more wood or supplies. They had done what they could, but the winter ahead was going to be a test of endurance for everyone.

Lillian sat at the counter, staring down at the ledger in front of her. The numbers were always the same, no matter how many times she tried to make them add up differently. She was running low on everything—food, supplies, money. And with winter on their heels, there wasn't much time left to figure out how to make it through.

She had spent the morning talking to Mrs. Granger, trying to swallow her pride long enough to ask for help. It wasn't something Lillian was used to—asking for help—but the weight of her responsibilities had become too much to bear alone.

"You're stronger than you think, child," Mrs. Granger had said, her sharp eyes softening slightly as she spoke. "But even the strong need help sometimes."

Lillian had nodded, though the tightness in her chest hadn't eased. She was grateful for Mrs. Granger's advice, but the fear of being unable to provide for Grace and Samuel weighed heavily on her.

She had been trying so hard to hold it all together, to be both mother and father to her children, but now, as the cold crept into every corner of their lives, she wasn't sure how much longer she could keep pretending everything was fine.

Later that afternoon, Nathan made his way to Riverside Boarding House, his shoulders heavy with the weight of the day. The repairs at the church had drained him physically and emotionally, and all he wanted was a moment of quiet—a moment to clear his head. But when he arrived at the boarding house, he found Rachel sitting on the front steps, her hands wrapped around a steaming cup of tea, her eyes distant.

She looked up as Nathan approached, her expression guarded but curious. "You're the one fixing the church, right?"

Nathan nodded, stopping a few feet away from her. "Yeah. Trying to, anyway."

Rachel smiled faintly, though it didn't reach her eyes. "Mrs. Granger told me about you. Said you're the quiet type."

Nathan shrugged. "I suppose I am." There was a brief silence, the cold wind whipping through the empty street as they stood there, uncertain how to navigate this moment.

Rachel had been in Millbrook for a few days now, but she still felt like an outsider, unsure if she belonged here. Nathan, in his own way, understood that feeling all too well.

"I wasn't planning to stay," Rachel said quietly, breaking the silence. "But… I don't know. This place… it feels different."

Nathan glanced at her, his dark eyes softening just slightly. "It's a hard place to leave."

Rachel met his gaze for a moment before looking away. "Maybe I'll stay," she murmured, almost as if she were saying it more to herself than to him. Nathan didn't respond, but there was a flicker of something like understanding between them—two people who had been running for too long, now finding themselves in a town that didn't ask for much but offered more than they had expected.

That night, Nathan lay in bed, his mind restless. The day had been long, the weight of everything pressing down on him like a stone. But as he drifted into a fitful sleep, his dreams turned dark.

In his nightmare, he was back at the river, but it wasn't calm this time. The water was rising, sweeping over him, pulling him under. Leslie was standing on the bank, her face filled with sorrow. Elizabeth was with her, but the water kept dragging him down no matter how hard Nathan tried to reach them. He couldn't breathe, couldn't speak—he was drowning, and there was nothing he could do to stop it.

He woke with a start, his heart racing, his breath coming in ragged gasps. The room was cold, the darkness pressing in around him, but the weight of the nightmare clung to him. The guilt, the grief—it was still there, lurking just beneath the surface, ready to pull him under.

The air was colder than usual the next morning. A biting chill seeped into Nathan's bones as he worked on the last of the repairs at the church. His hands were numb despite the gloves, and the cold wind seemed to cut right through his coat. The wood beneath his fingers felt solid, though, and that was something—at least the roof would hold.

The last few days had been hard, and Nathan could feel the tension building in the town. Everyone was on edge. Food was running low, winter was closing in fast, and the cracks were starting to show. Even Reverend James, usually the voice of hope, seemed weighed down by the burden of what was coming.

As Nathan hammered the final nail into place, he could hear the low murmur of conversation coming from below. Reverend James and Mayor Thornton stood near the entrance to the church, their voices quiet but tense. Nathan couldn't make out everything they were saying, but it was clear that they were at odds.

The mayor was pacing, his hands shoved into his coat pockets, his brow furrowed. "We need to be realistic, James," the mayor said, his voice carrying slightly in the cold air. "We don't have enough supplies to make it through the winter at this rate. If we don't start rationing now, we won't have anything left."

Reverend James shook his head, his expression firm but weary. "We can't give up on hope, John. The town needs to believe we can pull through this. If we start cutting people off now, we'll lose what little spirit we have left."

Mayor Thornton stopped pacing and turned to face the reverend. "I'm not talking about cutting people off. I'm talking about being smart. There are families here with children. We need to prioritize them."

Nathan paused in his work, his chest tightening at the mayor's words. He knew what was coming. The conversation was heading toward a place he had hoped to avoid—rationing food, cutting back on who received help, and leaving people like him, Rachel, and others who were seen as outsiders on the edge of survival.

"We've faced hard winters before, John," Reverend James said, his voice softer now. "We've always found a way through."

"This isn't like the others," the mayor replied, his voice low but firm. "We can't save everyone."

The words hung in the air like a cloud, thick and heavy. Nathan's grip on the hammer tightened, a surge of anger rising in his chest. Save everyone? He knew what the mayor meant—people like him didn't count. People who weren't from Millbrook and didn't have family ties weren't prioritized.

The weight of it all pressed down on him, and for a moment, he considered leaving again. Running. It was what he was good at—avoiding the mess, the decisions, the pain. But something kept him rooted there. His hands clenched around the hammer, his breath visible in the cold morning air.

Chapter Eighteen: The Breaking Point

The cold settled over Millbrook like a weight, pressing down on the town with an unforgiving chill. The wind howled through the narrow streets, and the sky hung heavy with gray clouds, threatening more snow before the night was through. It wasn't a blizzard by any means, but the roads were already slick with ice, and the steady fall of snow was enough to make travel dangerous.

Nathan stood on the church roof, his fingers stiff from the cold as he worked to finish the last repairs. The wind bit at his face, and the snow swirled lightly around him, collecting in small drifts along the edge of the roof. His breath came in short, visible puffs, and every muscle in his body ached from the hours of labor in the freezing conditions.

Below, Reverend James and Mayor Thornton stood at the entrance of the church, their faces drawn with worry. The storm wasn't as bad as it could have been, but it was enough to create real trouble for the town. The roads were becoming impassable, and the cold settled in deeper each day.

"We don't have enough food to last if this weather keeps up," Mayor Thornton muttered, his voice barely audible above the wind. "We should have rationed sooner."

Reverend James nodded. "We'll find a way through," he said, though his voice lacked the conviction it usually carried. "We always have."

The mayor sighed, pulling his coat tighter around him as the wind whipped through the church's open doorway.

"We need to make some tough decisions, James. We can't save everyone." Nathan's hands stilled for a moment as the words drifted to him, carried by the wind. Can't save everyone.

It was a refrain he had heard too many times, and each time, it cut deeper. He had thought about leaving Millbrook more than once since arriving, but something had kept him here. Maybe it was the people. Maybe it was the chance to make a difference, to stop running for once in his life. But now, as he climbed down from the roof, the mayor's words lingered in his mind. Can't save everyone.

"The roof will hold," Nathan said quietly as he joined the mayor and reverend at the church entrance. His voice was hoarse from the cold, his breath visible in the icy air. "It should get us through the winter."

Reverend James nodded, gratitude flickering in his tired eyes. "Thank you, Nathan. You've done more for this town than you realize."

Nathan didn't respond.

The wind whipped through the streets, carrying the weight of the storm and the unspoken fear that hung over the town like a cloud. The cold was only beginning, but the real threat wasn't the snow or the ice—it was what came after.

The long, harsh winter. The dwindling supplies. The choices people would have to make to survive.

At Thompson Supplies, Lillian stood by the window, watching as the snow fell in a steady, persistent sheet. The store was almost empty, the shelves bare except for a few scattered items. The firewood was running out, and there was no sign of a delivery truck making it through the icy roads anytime soon.

She had sent Grace and Samuel to the back room to keep warm, but her mind was elsewhere. She was trying to make the numbers in the ledger work, trying to figure out how to stretch the supplies they had left, but no matter how hard she tried, the numbers wouldn't add up. There wasn't enough food. There wasn't enough of anything.

Her heart pounded as she turned away from the window, her stomach twisting with worry. The cold seemed to seep through every crack in the walls, making it impossible to escape the chill. She had been holding everything together for so long, but now, with the icy roads and the growing fear in town, she wasn't sure how much longer she could keep going.

The loud crash behind her jolted her from her thoughts. She turned just in time to see one of the barrels of kerosene tip over, spilling its contents across the floor. Her pulse quickened as she rushed toward the mess, trying to contain it before it spread. But then it happened—before she could react, a spark ignited, and the kerosene went up in flames.

"Grace! Samuel!" Lillian screamed, panic flooding her as the flames spread across the floor, licking up the wooden shelves. "Get out! Now!"

The children froze, their eyes wide with fear, as the smoke began to fill the room. Lillian grabbed a nearby towel, trying to smother the flames, but they were growing too fast, the heat unbearable. Her heart pounded as she fought to contain the fire, but it was useless.

Just when she thought the fire would consume everything, the door burst open, and Nathan rushed inside. His face was pale from the cold, his eyes wide with shock as he took in the scene. Without a word, he grabbed a bucket of water from the back of the store, dousing the flames with quick, decisive movements. The fire sputtered out, leaving only smoke and the charred remnants of the store. Lillian collapsed against the counter, her breath coming in short, ragged gasps. Her hands were shaking, her chest tight with fear and relief.

"You okay?" Nathan asked, his voice low and steady as he knelt beside her. Lillian nodded, though tears welled up in her eyes.

"I... I couldn't... I didn't know what to do." Nathan's expression softened, his hand resting on her shoulder. "It's okay. It's over." But it wasn't over—not really. The fire had been put out, but the weight of everything else still hung over her. The cold. The lack of supplies. The fear of not being able to protect her children. It was all too much.

"I'm failing them," Lillian whispered, her voice breaking as the tears spilled. "I can't keep them safe. I can't…"

Nathan's grip on her shoulder tightened slightly, his eyes searching hers. "You're not failing them," he said quietly. "You're doing everything you can."

Lillian looked away, her chest aching with the weight of her fears. "I don't know how much longer I can do this."

Nathan didn't have an answer. He didn't know how to fix what was broken, but he didn't feel like running for the first time in a long time. He felt like staying.

The snow continued to fall throughout the day, turning the streets into slippery, dangerous paths. By the time the sun set, the roads were treacherous, and the cold was biting. But despite the storm, the town meeting went ahead as planned. People bundled up and trudged through the snow to the church, their faces lined with worry and fear. Inside, the air was thick with tension. Everyone knew the situation was dire, and the storm only worsened.

Mayor Thornton stood at the front of the room, his face grim as he addressed the crowd. "We're running out of time," the mayor began, his voice loud enough to carry over the sound of the wind that rattled the windows. "The storm is making everything harder, and our supplies are already low. We need to start rationing now."

The crowd murmured agreement, but the tension was palpable. People were scared. The cold had isolated them even more than they had already been, and now the reality of their situation was sinking in.

"We'll prioritize families with children," Mayor Thornton continued, his tone pragmatic. "But we'll do everything we can to make sure everyone gets something."

Nathan sat in the back of the church, his arms crossed over his chest as he listened. The cold had set everyone on edge, but the mayor's words truly unsettled him. Prioritize families. He knew what that meant—those who didn't have families and were seen as outsiders would be left with the scraps.

Before he could stop himself, Nathan stood, his voice breaking the tense silence in the room. "We can't leave people behind," he said, his voice firm. "We're all struggling. You can't just cut people off because they don't have families here."

The room fell silent, all eyes turning to Nathan.

Chapter Nineteen: Fractured Trust

The cold clung to Millbrook like a heavy blanket, and even as the storm eased, the snow and ice left the town almost suffocating in its isolation. The streets were quieter than usual, with only a few people braving the biting wind to walk through the snow-covered paths. Despite the apparent calm, an undercurrent of unease lingered a tension that crackled in the air.

Nathan moved through the streets, his boots sinking into the snow with each step, but it wasn't the cold that weighed on him—it was the whispers. Ever since the town meeting, he could feel the eyes of the townsfolk on him, their conversations stopping the moment he passed by. Outside the bakery, a group of men huddled together, their coats pulled tightly against the chill. The faint smell of bread drifted through the air, a rare and precious scent, given how little food remained in town.

Nathan slowed his pace as he overheard their conversation. "I don't see why we should be giving rations to those who just wandered in," one man muttered, his breath visible in the cold air. His face was red from the wind, and his expression was hard. "We barely have enough for our own families."

Another man, younger and less sure of himself, hesitated. "But he's been helping out, hasn't he? Fixing things up around town."

The older man scoffed. "So what? He fixes a roof or two, and suddenly, he deserves the same food as folks who've been here their whole lives. No, I say we look after our own first." Nathan's jaw clenched, but he kept his gaze forward, his pace steady.

He had heard it all in every town he'd passed through. When times get hard, people turn inward, protecting their own at the expense of anyone else. Outsiders were always the first to be cast aside, no matter how much they tried to help.

As he moved past Thompson Supplies, he caught sight of Lillian through the window. She was sitting behind the counter, her head resting in her hands, her face a mask of exhaustion. The store was nearly empty, with only a few remaining bags of grain and dried goods lining the shelves. Lillian had been forced to ration supplies strictly, and it was taking a toll on her physically and emotionally.

Nathan slowed as he watched her, feeling a pang of sympathy. She had always tried to be strong for her children and for the town, but even she was starting to buckle under the weight of it all. The cracks were showing.

At the blacksmith shop, the tension was just as palpable. Inside, the heat from the forge was intense, a sharp contrast to the biting cold outside. Ryan stood by the anvil, sweat dripping down his face as he swung the hammer, but each strike was weaker than the last. His grip faltered, and the hammer slipped from his hand, falling to the ground with a dull thud. Ryan cursed under his breath, bending down to retrieve the hammer, but his hand trembled from the effort.

"Ryan!" Earl barked from across the shop, his arms crossed over his chest. His voice was sharp, filled with a mixture of concern and frustration. "You're dragging today. We've got orders to fill out and are behind."

"I'm trying," Ryan shot back, his voice tight with frustration. He wiped the sweat from his brow, his face pale despite the heat from the forge. "But I'm not at full strength yet."

"You're not doing yourself any favors by pushing through the pain," Earl said, stepping forward. His tone softened slightly, but there was still an edge of impatience. "You've got to heal, Ryan. If you keep going like this, you'll only worsen it."

Ryan's hands tightened around the hammer, his knuckles white. "I don't have a choice," he muttered. "If I don't work, I'm no good to anyone."

"You're no good to anyone if you collapse in the middle of the shop," Earl said firmly. "I get it—you don't want to sit around and feel useless. But pushing yourself too hard now will only make things worse later."

Ryan's shoulders slumped, the weight of Earl's words sinking in. "I just… I don't want to be a burden."

Earl's expression softened, and he firmly touched Ryan's shoulder. "You're not a burden, kid. You've been through enough. Take the time you need to heal. We'll manage."

Ryan nodded slowly, though the frustration in his eyes remained. Earl's words had hit home, but it was clear that Ryan was struggling with the feeling of helplessness, the sense that he wasn't contributing enough. And in a town like Millbrook, where every able-bodied person was needed to survive, that feeling weighed heavily.

Later that afternoon, Nathan was drawn to the edge of town, where the snow-dusted woods created a quiet, almost serene landscape. The sky had cleared slightly, though the biting cold remained, and the only sounds were the crunch of snow beneath his boots and the distant rustling of the wind through the trees.

As he neared the Riverside Boarding House, he spotted Rachel standing alone by the tree line, her arms wrapped around herself as if trying to shield herself from more than just the cold. Her expression was distant, her gaze fixed on something far beyond the horizon.

Nathan approached her slowly, his breath visible in the icy air. "Rachel," he called softly.

She turned to his voice, her eyes flickering with recognition. "Nathan," she said her voice barely above a whisper. "I didn't hear you coming."

He stopped beside her, his brow furrowing with concern. "You alright? You look… distant."

Rachel's eyes drifted back toward the woods, and for a long moment, she said nothing. Finally, she let out a shaky breath. "I've been thinking about leaving," she admitted, her voice heavy with uncertainty.

The words caught Nathan off guard, and for a moment, he didn't know how to respond. "Leaving?" he echoed. "Why?"

Rachel sighed, her breath clouding in the cold air. "It's not safe for me here," she said quietly. "Not with him looking for me. If he finds me… I'm putting everyone at risk by staying."

Nathan stepped closer, his concern deepening. "You're not putting anyone at risk. We can protect you."

Rachel shook her head, her eyes filled with doubt. "You don't understand. He's not the kind of man you can scare off. He's… dangerous. He always finds me. And when he does… people get hurt."

Nathan's jaw tightened, a surge of anger rising in his chest at the thought of someone hurting Rachel. "You don't have to run," he said, his voice low but firm. "Not anymore. You've been running your whole life, and I get it—I've done the same. But this time… this time you stay."

Rachel blinked back the tears that threatened to fall, her voice trembling. "I don't want to run, Nathan. I'm tired. But I don't know how to stop."

Nathan reached out, gently resting a hand on her shoulder. "You don't have to do it alone," he said softly. "We'll figure this out. Together."

For a long moment, they stood in silence, the snow falling gently around them. Rachel's face was pale, her eyes shadowed with fear, but something in Nathan's words seemed to reach her. "I don't want to be a burden," she whispered, her voice barely audible.

"You're not," Nathan said, his voice steady. "We take care of each other here. That's what a community does."

Rachel looked up at him, her eyes searching his for any sign of doubt. But all she saw was sincerity, and slowly nodded, though the fear remained.

Chapter Twenty: Faith in the Storm

The first Sunday of December arrived with a biting cold that seeped through every crack and crevice in Millbrook. Snow covered the ground in a thin, frozen layer, and the wind whipped sharply through the streets, carrying the scent of pine and frost. The town seemed quieter than usual as if the cold itself had frozen the air.

But in the heart of Millbrook, the small, weathered church stood as a beacon of warmth and refuge. The people of the town shuffled through the doors, their coats pulled tight around them, their breath visible in the cold air as they greeted one another with hushed voices. Inside, the church was dimly lit, the smell of old wood and candle wax filling the space, while the faint glow of the hearth in the corner fought back the winter chill. The pews creaked as families took their places, and the faint rustling of coats and scarves filled the air.

Nathan sat toward the back, as he often did, his shoulders hunched against the cold that seemed to linger even inside the church. His eyes scanned the room, noticing how the faces of the townspeople were thinner, their expressions wearier. It had been a week since the rationing had begun, and though the snow had eased, the hunger had only grown. Stomachs were emptier, and tempers were shorter.

In the front pew, Lillian sat with Samuel and Grace. She adjusted Grace's coat, her fingers trembling slightly as she pulled the fabric tight around her daughter's thin frame. Samuel sat quietly beside her, his face serious and still, as though the weight of their circumstances had already begun to settle on his young shoulders. Lillian's mind was elsewhere, though—her thoughts on the growing hunger in the town and the dwindling supplies at Thompson Supplies. The sermon hadn't even begun, but already she felt the crushing weight of her responsibilities pressing down on her.

As the church bell tolled softly, Reverend James stepped up to the front, his worn Bible in hand, and the congregation slowly quieted. His eyes, though tired, held a glimmer of warmth as he looked out at the people gathered before him.

"Brothers and sisters," he began, his voice low and steady, "we are facing trials that test us in ways we've never known. The hunger, the cold—it wears on our spirits as much as it wears on our bodies. But I ask you today to remember that we are called to persevere in times of hardship."

Nathan shifted in his seat, his arms crossed tightly over his chest. The word persevere felt like a weight in his mind, an expectation he wasn't sure he could meet. He'd been running from hardship for so long that the idea of staying put—of enduring—was foreign to him.

The faces of Leslie and Elizabeth flickered in his mind, ghosts he couldn't shake, and for a moment, he wanted nothing more than to walk out of the church and keep running. But something kept him rooted in his seat. Reverend James opened his Bible, his fingers tracing the worn pages as he read aloud from James 1:12: "Blessed is the one who perseveres under trial because, having stood the test, that person will receive the crown of life that the Lord has promised to those who love him."

Nathan's jaw tightened. Perseverance. Standing the test. He didn't feel blessed. He felt broken, weighed down by guilt and grief that he couldn't seem to shake. The reverend's words echoed in his ears, but part of him felt like they weren't meant for him. How could he receive any sort of blessing when he had failed the people he loved most?

In the front row, Lillian tried to focus on the reverend's words, but her mind kept drifting back to Samuel and Grace. They were so quiet lately, their faces growing thinner each day, the hunger gnawing at them even though she tried her best to stretch the food. She glanced at Grace, who was fidgeting beside her, her small hands clutched tightly around the edges of her coat. The girl's stomach had been rumbling all morning, and Lillian felt the familiar ache of helplessness settle in her chest. Reverend James's voice broke through her thoughts.

"When the weight of the world feels too heavy, remember that you are not carrying it alone. The Lord walks with you, even in the darkest of times."

Lillian swallowed hard, her eyes stinging with unshed tears. She wanted to believe that—she wanted to believe that God was with her, that He was watching over her children. But every day felt like another battle, and she was running out of strength.

    Rachel sat near the middle of the congregation, her hands folded tightly in her lap, her eyes focused on the floor. The reverend's words washed over her, but she felt distant, as though she were watching everything from the outside. The weight of her past still pressed down on her, and every day, she considered leaving Millbrook. She thought of the man who was looking for her, the fear that clung to her like a shadow, and she wondered if she could ever truly be safe. But something inside her shifted as she listened to the reverend speak of perseverance. The idea of standing the test and not running was foreign to her, but maybe, just maybe, there was a way forward. Maybe staying in Millbrook was the bravest thing she could do.

    Near the back of the church, Earl sat with his arms crossed over his chest, his weathered face unreadable. The reverend's words stirred memories of winters past, of times when the town had been through hard seasons, and somehow, they had made it through. He glanced around the congregation, his eyes landing on Ryan, who sat quietly beside Mrs. Granger. The boy still looked pale, his injury slowing him down, and Earl felt a surge of protectiveness. He had taken Ryan under his wing and wasn't about to let the kid fall behind. The reverend's voice softened.

"The trials we face now will test us, but they will not break us. We are stronger together, and through God's grace, we will endure."

Earl nodded slightly to himself. They would get through this—he had no doubt about that. It wouldn't be easy, but Millbrook had survived hard times before. He just needed to make sure he did his part to keep things running smoothly.

The sermon ended with a soft prayer, and as the congregation rose from their seats, a heavy silence hung in the air. The service touched everyone in different ways; the message of perseverance resonated deeply, but the reality of their situation—hunger and cold—remained.

Nathan lingered at the back of the church, watching as the families slowly filed out, their faces drawn with weariness. Lillian was gathering Samuel and Grace, her hands moving quickly as she adjusted their scarves and coats, her brow furrowed with worry. He hadn't spoken to her much since the fire, but something inside him urged him forward.

"Lillian," he called softly as he approached her. She looked up, her expression surprised but not unfriendly.

"Nathan." "Everything alright?" he asked, though he could see from the lines of exhaustion on her face that things were anything but.

Lillian hesitated, glancing down at her children before answering. "It's… as alright as it can be. The kids are holding up."

Nathan nodded, though the words felt heavy. "If you need anything… just let me know."

Lillian gave him a small, tired smile. "Thank you. I appreciate that."

As they stood there, the cold air swirling around them, there was a moment of quiet understanding between them—both of them carrying burdens that felt too heavy, but somehow, in that brief exchange, the weight seemed a little lighter.

Rachel, meanwhile, found herself standing beside Mrs. Granger after the service. The older woman gave her a kind smile, her eyes soft and understanding. "You've got a lot on your mind, dear."

Rachel nodded slowly. "I… I think I'm going to stay," she said, the words feeling both terrifying and liberating at the same time. "I don't want to run anymore."

Mrs. Granger's smile widened, and she placed a comforting hand on Rachel's arm. "You've made the right choice, child. Millbrook's a good place. You'll be safe here."

Rachel wasn't entirely sure she believed that, but she felt a small flicker of hope for the first time in a long while.

As the townspeople gathered their things and exited the church, the air outside felt colder and sharper. The snow crunched beneath their feet as they walked back to their homes, their hearts a little lighter from the message they had received.

But the hunger remained, gnawing at their stomachs, a reminder of their hardships. Inside the church, Reverend James stood by the door, his hands clasped in quiet prayer as the last of the congregation left. He knew that the week ahead would be hard, that the rationing and the cold would test the town's limits. But as he looked out over the snow-covered streets, he held onto the hope that his message had given the people of Millbrook something to hold onto—something to carry them through the storm.

Chapter Twenty-One: Struggles in the Cold

The wind howled outside the church, shaking the old wooden structure like an autumn leaf caught in a storm. The faint glow from the hearth barely pushed back the deep chill settling into the small room.

Nathan sat stiffly on one of the pews, his elbows resting on his knees, his hands clasped tightly in front of him. His shoulders were hunched, and his eyes fixed on the floor as though he couldn't bear to meet the gaze of the man sitting beside him.

Reverend James watched him quietly, his worn Bible resting on his lap, the edges of its pages softened from years of use. The reverend's face was gentle, his dark eyes patient and kind, the way only someone who had weathered their storms could be. The wind rattled the windows, but inside the church, the air was thick with the weight of words that had not yet been spoken.

Nathan had been sitting there for what felt like hours, though it had only been minutes. The silence between them stretched long and heavy like a rope pulled tight and ready to snap. He had come to the church to talk—of finally unburdening himself of the guilt that had been gnawing at him for years—but now that he was here, the words refused to come.

"You've been carrying a heavy burden, Nathan," Reverend James said softly, breaking the silence with his steady voice.

Nathan shifted, his fingers tightening around each other as his brow furrowed. "I don't know how to let it go," he admitted, his voice hoarse.

The reverend nodded, his gaze calm and understanding. "Sometimes we hold onto things because we fear what will happen if we let them go. But guilt… guilt can be a prison."

Nathan's breath caught in his throat. The reverend's words hit too close to home. For years, he had built walls around his pain, keeping it locked inside where no one could reach it. But those walls had also kept him trapped. He ran a hand through his dark hair, releasing a shaky breath.

"It's my fault," he whispered, his voice barely audible over the crackling of the fire. "Leslie… she was grieving, and I wasn't there for her. Not after Elizabeth…" His words trailed off, and the memories came rushing back like floodwaters breaching a dam.

He could see it so clearly—the way Leslie had stood by their daughter's grave, her face hollow with grief, her arms wrapped around herself as if she were trying to hold her shattered heart together.

He had been there, physically, but emotionally… emotionally, he had been drowning in his guilt. And in that moment, he had failed her. "I couldn't save her," Nathan whispered, his voice cracking. "Elizabeth died, and I couldn't save her. And then Leslie… she—"

His voice broke, and he fell silent, his chest heaving with the weight of his emotions. He could still see the wreckage, the twisted metal, the way the world had seemed to stop the day Leslie died in the car crash.

It was as if he had lost both of them in one fell swoop, and in the aftermath, all that had remained was guilt.

"I wasn't there for her," he said, his voice thick with emotion. "I couldn't be there for Leslie because I was too caught up in my own pain. I've been running ever since."

Reverend James listened quietly, his hands resting gently on his Bible, his gaze never leaving Nathan's face. When Nathan fell silent, the reverend waited for a moment before speaking.

"Grief is a heavy burden, Nathan," he said softly, his voice full of compassion. "It can blind us, making us believe we're alone in our suffering. But guilt… guilt isn't where you're meant to stay."

Nathan let out a bitter laugh, shaking his head. "It feels like it's all I have left." The reverend's eyes softened, and he opened his Bible, flipping through the pages until he found what he sought.

His fingers traced the familiar text, and his voice was full of quiet strength when he spoke. "Isaiah 43:18-19," he began, reading aloud: "Forget the former things; do not dwell on the past. See, I am doing a new thing! Now it springs up;

do you not perceive it? I am making a way in the wilderness and streams in the wasteland."

The words hung between them, and Nathan felt something shift inside him. The weight in his chest didn't disappear, but it felt... lighter. It was as if there was a flicker of hope for the first time in years—just a flicker, but enough to be felt.

"You've been lost in your own wilderness for a long time," Reverend James said gently. "But it's not too late to find your way out. God doesn't leave us where we are. He calls us forward."

Nathan swallowed hard, the tightness in his throat making it difficult to speak. "What if I don't deserve it?" he whispered. "What if it's too late for me?"

The reverend's eyes were full of understanding. "It's never too late, Nathan. Redemption isn't about what we deserve—it's about grace. And grace doesn't have a time limit."

Nathan closed his eyes, the words sinking deep into his heart. For so long, he had believed that his guilt was the only thing left of his past. But now, sitting in the quiet church, with the reverend's voice speaking truth into the darkness, he wondered if maybe—just maybe—there was a way forward.

Meanwhile, across town, Lillian sat at the kitchen table in Riverside Boarding House, her hands gripping a cup of tea that had long since gone cold. Mrs. Granger sat across from her, knitting needles resting beside her, her gaze soft and full of concern as she watched the younger woman wrestle with her emotions. The wind outside howled through the streets, rattling the windows and adding to the already tense atmosphere.

Inside, the warmth of the fire did little to ease the chill that had settled into Lillian's bones. "I don't know how much longer I can do this," Lillian said quietly, her voice trembling. "I'm trying... I'm doing everything I can, but it doesn't feel like enough. The shop, the kids... I'm barely keeping my head above water."

Mrs. Granger's eyes softened as she reached out, placing her hand over Lillian's. "You're doing more than enough, dear. You're holding your family together in the middle of the worst hardship any of us have known. That's not something to take lightly."

Lillian shook her head, her eyes filling with unshed tears. "But what if I can't keep doing it? What if I can't protect Samuel and Grace? There's less food and warmth every day, and I'm failing them. I can see it in their faces—they're hungry, and I can't give them what they need."

Her voice broke, and she quickly wiped away the tears from her cheeks. The weight of responsibility had been pressing down on her for weeks, and now, sitting in Mrs. Granger's warm kitchen, it felt as though the dam had finally broken.

Mrs. Granger squeezed her hand gently, her own heart aching for Lillian. "You are not failing them," she said softly. "You're doing everything you can, and that's what matters. No one is expecting you to carry this burden alone."

Lillian let out a shaky breath, her hands trembling as she set the cup of tea on the table. "But I am alone. I'm supposed to be the one holding it all together, but I'm falling apart. What kind of mother does that make me?"

Mrs. Granger's expression was full of understanding as she leaned forward, her voice low but steady. "It makes you human, Lillian. You're a mother, yes, but you're also a woman. You have limits, and it's okay to admit when you need help."

Lillian blinked back more tears, her heart heavy with the weight of her doubts. "I don't want to lose them," she whispered. "You won't,"

Mrs. Granger said firmly, her voice filled with quiet certainty. "Not while you're still fighting for them. You're stronger than you think, Lillian. And when you need to lean on someone, you lean on us. We're all in this together."

For the first time in days, Lillian allowed herself to believe those words. The weight on her shoulders didn't disappear, but in Mrs. Granger's steady presence, she felt a glimmer of hope—just enough to keep going.

Outside, the snow crunched beneath Rachel's boots as she walked alongside Nathan, the two of them moving through the narrow streets that lined the edge of town. The sky above them was pale and gray, and the wind whipped at their coats, sending shivers down their spines. Rachel kept her gaze fixed on the ground, her brow furrowed as she wrestled with her thoughts.

For weeks, she had kept her secrets hidden behind the walls she had built to protect herself. But now, as she walked beside Nathan, the walls were beginning to crack.

Chapter Twenty-Two: A New Hope

Rachel fixed her gaze on the ground, her brow furrowed as she wrestled with her thoughts. For weeks, she had kept her secrets hidden behind the walls she had built to protect herself. But now, as she walked beside Nathan, the walls were beginning to crack.

"I've been running for so long," she finally said, her voice barely audible over the wind. "Maybe if I kept moving and never stayed in one place too long, he wouldn't find me."

Nathan glanced at her, his expression soft but serious. He had sensed there was something Rachel had been holding back—something deeper than just the fear of survival during the harsh winter.

"Who is he?" he asked gently, though he could already guess the answer.

Rachel let out a shaky breath, her hands trembling as she clutched her coat tighter around herself. "My husband," she admitted quietly. "I thought… I thought he would change. I thought things would get better. But they didn't."

Her voice was thick with emotion, and Nathan could see the weight of her words, the years of running, of hiding. He remained silent, waiting for her to continue, knowing that pushing her would only make her retreat further into herself.

"We were married young," Rachel went on, her voice distant, as if she were talking about someone else's life. "At first, it wasn't so bad. He was... he could be charming when he wanted to be. But that was just part of it. The rest of the time, he was cruel. Controlling. Violent." Her voice wavered, and she swallowed hard as if trying to keep the memories from overwhelming her. "It took me a long time to realize that he wasn't going to change."

Nathan's heart clenched at the pain in her voice, and he felt an anger rise within him—not just toward her husband, but at the world that had allowed her to suffer for so long.

"You don't have to talk about it if you don't want to," he said gently, though he could sense that she needed to get it out.

"I finally left," Rachel continued, her voice trembling. "I ran. I didn't know where I was going—I just knew I had to escape him. But no matter how far I ran, he always found me. He always finds me."

Her words were filled with a deep sense of fear, and Nathan could see how much that fear had shaped her life. The way she kept to herself, the way she seemed always to be looking over her shoulder—it all made sense now.

"He's been looking for me," Rachel whispered, her eyes filled with unshed tears. "And I'm scared... I'm scared he'll find me again."

Nathan stopped walking, turning to face her, his expression serious and full of concern.

"Rachel, you're safe here," he said firmly. "I won't let anything happen to you." Rachel's eyes widened slightly as if she couldn't believe what she was hearing. "How can you be sure?" she asked, her voice filled with doubt. "How can anyone stop him?"

Nathan reached out, gently resting a hand on her shoulder. "I don't know," he admitted honestly. "But I do know that running hasn't helped you. And you're not alone anymore. You've got me, and you've got the rest of the town. We'll protect you."

Rachel looked up at him, her eyes searching his as if trying to find some reassurance that he wasn't just saying those words to comfort her. And in his gaze, she saw something she hadn't felt in a long time—hope.

"I don't want to be a burden," she whispered, her voice barely audible.

"You're not a burden," Nathan said softly but firmly. "You're part of this town now, and we take care of our own. You don't have to keep running."

For a long moment, Rachel was silent, her breath coming out in small, visible puffs in the cold air. Slowly, she nodded, though her fear still lingered in the corners of her mind. But there was something about Nathan's words—about his quiet strength—that made her want to believe that maybe, just maybe, she could stop running.

"Thank you," she whispered, her voice thick with emotion.

Nathan nodded, his expression softening as he let his hand fall back to his side. "You don't have to face this alone anymore," he said gently. "We'll get through this together."

As they continued walking, the snow crunching beneath their boots, Rachel felt a strange sense of peace. The fear wasn't gone—it would take time for that to fade—but she didn't feel so alone for the first time in years. She had spent so long-running and hiding that the idea of staying—of being part of a community—was terrifying and comforting.

They walked in silence; the wind whipped at their coats, but it wasn't an uncomfortable silence. It was the kind of quiet that came when two people understood each other when words weren't necessary. As they neared the edge of town, where the lights from the houses grew dimmer and the river whispered through the snow-covered banks, Nathan glanced at Rachel once more.

"You're stronger than you think," he said quietly, his voice carrying over the sound of the wind.

Rachel looked at him, her dark hair blowing in the wind, her eyes wide and vulnerable. For a moment, she didn't know what to say. But then she smiled—a small, hesitant smile, but a smile nonetheless. "Maybe," she said softly, though she wasn't quite ready to believe it. "Maybe."

Chapter Twenty-Three: Building and Mending

The cold air seeped into the cracks of Thompson Supplies, making the shop feel more like a freezer than a place of business. Lillian stood by the window, her breath visible in the frosty air as she wrapped her arms tightly around herself. The winter had taken its toll on everything—the store, her family, and the town—but today, her concern was focused on the building that had sheltered her and her children for so long.

Nathan stepped through the front door, stomping the snow off his boots as he entered the store's state. The roof had sprung a leak during the last storm, and several boards along the side of the building were beginning to rot. The shelves inside were sparse, filled with only the barest essentials, and the creak of the floorboards underfoot added to the shop's sense of weariness.

"Looks like I came just in time," Nathan said, his voice steady as he took off his coat and rolled up his sleeves. Lillian offered him a tired smile.

"I don't know how much longer this place can hold up without falling apart," she admitted her voice soft but tinged with worry.

Nathan grabbed his tools and nodded toward the roof. "I'll start on the leak," he said. "Shouldn't take too long to patch it up."

As Nathan climbed onto the roof, Lillian watched from below, her heart heavy. She hated feeling helpless, but she couldn't deny that Nathan's presence had been a comfort since he had arrived in Millbrook. He worked without complaint, and despite his own demons, he seemed to find solace in the physical labor.

Lillian busied herself organizing the shelves, trying to keep her mind off of the fact that they were running low on almost everything. The rhythmic sound of Nathan hammering echoed through the store, a steady reminder that things were, at least at this moment, getting fixed. But Lillian's thoughts were far from settled. As she rearranged the cans on the shelves, she could feel the weight of her worries pressing down on her. The store was just a building, but it represented so much more than that—her livelihood, her children's future, her own sense of survival.

After what felt like hours, Nathan climbed down from the roof, wiping the sweat from his brow despite the cold. "That should hold for a while," he said, glancing up at the patched section.

"Thank you," Lillian said, her voice quiet. "I don't know what I'd do without your help."

Nathan shook his head, dismissing her gratitude with a wave of his hand. "You don't have to thank me," he said. "It's just a patch job."

But Lillian wasn't talking about the roof, and Nathan seemed to sense it. He looked at her, his dark eyes steady, and for a moment, the weight of everything unsaid hung between them. Lillian let out a slow breath, turning back to the shelves.

"I'm scared, Nathan," she admitted, her voice barely above a whisper. "I'm scared I can't provide for my kids. Every day it feels like there's less food, less money, less hope."

Nathan paused, his gaze softening as he watched her. He knew that feeling all too well—the crushing fear that comes from being responsible for others and not knowing if you can keep them safe.

"You're doing everything you can," Nathan said quietly, stepping closer. "You're holding this place together, even when everything around you is falling apart. That's more than most people can say."

Lillian's shoulders slumped as she leaned against the counter, her eyes filling with unshed tears. "But what if it's not enough?" she whispered, her voice breaking. "What if I can't do it anymore?"

Nathan reached out, resting a hand on her shoulder. "You're not alone in this," he said softly. "You've got Samuel, Grace… and you've got me. We'll get through this."

The touch of his hand, gentle and reassuring, sent a wave of warmth through Lillian's cold body. For a brief moment, she allowed herself to lean into his presence, finding comfort in the strength of his words.

She hadn't realized just how much she needed to hear that she wasn't alone. As they stood there, a quiet understanding passed between them. It wasn't romantic—at least not yet—but it was the kind of connection that grows when two people face hardships together.

They were both fighting battles, trying to survive in a world that seemed determined to break them. And in that shared struggle, they found a sense of kinship that neither of them had expected.

Rachel stood in the shadow of the store's doorway, watching the scene unfold between Nathan and Lillian. Her heart twisted in ways she hadn't expected as she observed the quiet exchange. Nathan's kindness and willingness to help were part of what drew her to him in the first place. But seeing him with Lillian—a woman who had known her share of loss and hardship—stirred feelings Rachel hadn't prepared for. She had been running for so long, unsure of where she fit in the world, and now, seeing Nathan and Lillian together, she couldn't help but wonder if she had found her place too late.

She wasn't jealous, not exactly, but there was a pang of something close to it—a fear that maybe she was too broken, too damaged to ever have what Lillian seemed to be finding with Nathan.

Rachel turned away before they could see her, the cold wind biting at her cheeks as she returned to the boarding house. The snow crunched beneath her boots, the sound sharp in the quiet of the morning, and her mind raced with thoughts she couldn't quite make sense of.

Later that afternoon, as Nathan continued to work on the repairs, Reverend James passed by the store, his face weary but kind. "I see you're putting in some hard work today, Nathan," the reverend said with a smile.

"Just trying to help where I can," Nathan replied, stepping down from the ladder and wiping his hands on his pants. Reverend James nodded, glancing around the nearly empty shelves inside the store. "The town's holding on, but just barely," he said quietly. "The cold's getting worse, and people are starting to worry about how long the food will last."

Nathan's jaw tightened as he glanced back toward Lillian, who was still busy inside the shop. "I know," he said. "Lillian's been running herself ragged trying to keep this place going."

The reverend sighed, his breath visible in the cold air. "We're all feeling the strain. The rationing's been hard on everyone, and I've been hearing rumors that some folks are starting to hoard supplies."

Nathan frowned. "Hoarding?" Reverend James nodded. "People are scared, Nathan. When fear takes over, people start thinking of themselves first. It's understandable, but it makes things harder for everyone." As they spoke, a commotion from down the street caught their attention.

Two men were arguing loudly, their voices carrying over the wind. Nathan exchanged a glance with the reverend before making his way toward the noise, his heart sinking as he recognized the familiar face of Earl, the town's blacksmith, standing toe-to-toe with Jed, one of the town's farmers.

"I know you've been holding back grain, Jed!" Earl shouted, his face red with anger. "People are starving, and you've got enough to feed your family twice over!"

"I've got kids to feed!" Jed shot back, his voice filled with desperation. "You don't know what it's like to see your children go to bed hungry!"

Nathan stepped between them before the argument could escalate further. "Both of you need to calm down," he said firmly, placing a hand on Earl's chest to keep him from advancing. "We're all in this together, remember?"

Earl clenched his fists, his eyes burning with frustration, but he backed down, though the tension still hung thick in the air.

Reverend James stepped forward, his voice calm but authoritative. "This isn't how we survive, folks. Fighting amongst ourselves will only make things worse."

The crowd that had gathered murmured in agreement, though the anger and fear were still palpable. As the argument died down, Nathan felt the weight of the town's struggles pressing down on him. Fixing the roof was one thing, but the deeper cracks in the community were harder to mend.

That evening, as the sun dipped below the horizon and the cold settled even deeper over Millbrook, Nathan stood outside the store, looking out over the snow-covered streets. The repairs had been finished, but the work was far from over. There was still so much brokenness that needed to be fixed, not just in the town but in the hearts of the people who lived there. He glanced back at the store, where Lillian was closing for the night. They had made it through another day, but the question that lingered in Nathan's mind was how many more days like this they could survive.

Chapter Twenty-Four: Shadows of the Past

Reverend James came walking down the street, his coat pulled tightly around him, his face etched with concern.

"Nathan, Lillian," he called out, quickening his pace as he approached. "There's something you need to hear."

"What's going on?" Nathan asked, stepping forward, sensing that whatever news the reverend brought wasn't good.

The reverend stopped in front of them, catching his breath. "Mayor Thornton's called a meeting at the church tonight. There's trouble brewing. People are getting nervous—more nervous than usual. There's talk that some folks have been hoarding supplies."

"Hoarding?" Lillian's brow furrowed, her grip tightening on the broom. "Who's saying that?"

Reverend James shook his head. "I don't know exactly, but rumors are spreading, and you know how fear makes people act. The mayor wants to address it before things get out of hand."

Nathan glanced at Lillian. The town had been holding on by a thread since the rationing began. With winter bearing down on them, the scarcity of food and supplies had everyone on edge. A conflict over hoarding could be the spark that tore the town apart.

"I'll be there," Nathan said firmly. "If things start to go south, I can help keep the peace."

Reverend James nodded, clearly relieved. "Thank you. We need to remind folks that we're all in this together—especially with Christmas coming and no sign of things getting easier."

Rachel stood by the window of the Riverside Boarding House, her hands gripping the windowsill as she stared out at the snow-covered streets. She could see Nathan and Lillian talking with the reverend across the way, their faces serious. Her heart tightened at the sight—not because of the trouble brewing in the town but because of the connection she saw growing between them. Rachel knew she had no right to feel this way. After all, she wasn't even using her real name.

She had left that behind when she fled from her husband, running as far as she could. But here, in Millbrook, for the first time in years, she had felt something close to peace—a fragile hope that she could build a new life. But seeing Nathan and Lillian together stirred something in her that she didn't want to acknowledge. She had seen how Lillian looked at Nathan and how Nathan stayed close to her as he worked. Rachel felt out of place, her carefully constructed walls starting to crack.

A knock at the door startled her, pulling her from her thoughts. Her heart jumped into her throat. For a moment, irrational fear gripped her, her mind flashing back to all the times she had heard a knock and feared it was him—her husband—coming to take her back.

"Rachel?" Mrs. Granger's voice came from the other side of the door, gentle but familiar. "Are you alright, dear?"

Rachel exhaled shakily, forcing herself to relax. She opened the door, offering a weak smile. "I'm fine," she said, though the tightness in her chest told a different story.

Mrs. Granger studied her with a knowing look. "You don't look fine," she said softly, setting her basket of knitting supplies on the small table. "You've been distant lately. Is something on your mind?"

Rachel hesitated, her mind racing. She wanted to confide in Mrs. Granger, to tell her the truth, but the words caught in her throat. She had spent so long running—building her new identity as "Rachel"—that admitting the truth now felt like giving up.

"I've just been thinking," Rachel said finally, her voice quieter now. "About the town, the supplies. I heard there's a meeting tonight."

Mrs. Granger nodded, her expression softening. "Yes, Mayor Thornton's called it. People are scared, but we'll get through this. We've survived worse."

Rachel nodded, but her mind wasn't on the meeting. It was on the whispers she had overheard at the market earlier that week—rumors of a man passing through nearby towns, asking questions. The knot in her stomach tightened, and she wondered if it was him—if her husband had found her again.

"I heard rumors," Rachel said, her voice barely above a whisper. "About a man asking questions. Do you think… do you think he's looking for someone?"

Mrs. Granger frowned slightly, concern deepening in her gaze. "It's hard to say, dear. But you're safe here in Millbrook." Rachel wanted to believe that—wanted to believe she was safe here. But the fear gnawing at her refused to be silenced. Deep down, she knew her past was never far behind.

By the time the meeting began at the church, the tension in the air was thick. The small room was packed with townspeople, their faces drawn tight with worry. Nathan stood near the back, arms crossed as he scanned the crowd. Lillian stood beside him, her expression guarded, while Rachel sat further back, her heart pounding as the meeting began.

Mayor Thornton, tall and commanding with his usual no-nonsense demeanor, stood at the front of the room, waiting for the murmurs to die down. When the room was quiet enough, he cleared his throat.

"We all know times are hard," Mayor Thornton began, his voice even and measured. "But we're in this together. There's been talk—rumors—that some of us aren't playing fair when it comes to supplies."

The tension in the room thickened as people exchanged glances.

Earl, the blacksmith, was the first to speak up. "I've heard there's grain going missing. Someone's stockpiling." All eyes turned toward Jed, the farmer, who stood stiffly near the front.

"I'm doing the best I can," Jed snapped. "I've got a family to feed too."

Nathan shifted uncomfortably, sensing that the conversation was about to spiral.

"We're all doing our best," Mayor Thornton said, raising a hand to calm the rising tension. "But we need to be careful. If we start turning on each other, this town won't make it through the winter."

Jed's face reddened, his voice trembling as he continued. "And what if I'm protecting my family? There's a stranger asking questions in nearby towns—looking for a woman. I'm not taking chances with my family."

Rachel's blood ran cold. A stranger. Asking questions. Her heart pounded in her chest, and the room seemed to close in around her. Nathan caught the change in her expression and stepped closer. "Rachel…"

"I need to go," she whispered, standing abruptly. Her hands trembled as she made her way toward the door.

Nathan followed her outside, the cold air biting at their skin. "Rachel, wait."

She stopped just outside the church, the snow falling softly around them, her breath coming in sharp bursts. "He's found me," she whispered, her voice breaking. "He's here. He's looking for me."

Nathan stepped closer, his voice calm and steady. "We don't know that for sure."

Rachel shook her head, tears welling in her eyes. "I can't stay. I can't put you all in danger."

"You're not leaving," Nathan said firmly, his hands gently gripping her shoulders. "We'll figure this out. You don't have to run anymore."

Rachel's breath caught in her throat as she looked up at him, her heart racing. She had spent so long-running and hiding, but now, standing here with Nathan, she wasn't sure she could keep running anymore.

Before she could respond, the church door creaked open, and Lillian stepped out into the cold. She looked between Nathan and Rachel, her brow furrowed with concern. "Is everything alright?" Lillian asked, her voice soft but edged with worry.

Rachel quickly wiped at her eyes, trying to compose herself. "I... I'm fine," she lied, though the tremor in her voice was unmistakable. "Just needed some air."

Lillian didn't push, but her eyes remained on Nathan as if silently asking him to explain. Nathan gave her a small nod, a quiet reassurance that he had the situation under control.

"You should come back inside," Lillian said gently, looking at Rachel with a mixture of kindness and uncertainty. "The meeting's still going on."

Rachel nodded slowly, though her heart still pounded in her chest. The fear of being found—of her past catching up to her—was overwhelming. But there was something about the way Nathan had spoken to her, the quiet confidence in his voice, that made her feel like, just maybe, she could stop running.

"We'll talk about this later," Nathan said softly as they moved toward the church door. "You're not alone in this, Rachel."

She didn't respond, but her eyes met his, and for a moment, the weight of her fear seemed to lessen, if only just. As they stepped back into the warmth of the church, the murmurs of the townspeople filled the room. Mayor Thornton was still at the front, trying to calm the tension between the crowd.

The accusations of hoarding hadn't died down, and the room crackled with a mix of frustration and fear.

"Let's not forget," Mayor Thornton's voice rang out, his deep tone commanding attention, "we survive as a community. If we let fear tear us apart, we're doomed."

Nathan exchanged a glance with Lillian. The town was on edge, and he knew that things could easily spiral out of control. As the meeting continued, Nathan's mind was half on the words being spoken and half on Rachel—on the look in her eyes when she had told him that someone was looking for her.

The meeting finally came to a close with promises of more discussions about rationing, but the unease among the townspeople remained thick. As people filed out into the cold, Nathan lingered at the back of the church, his eyes following Rachel as she quietly slipped toward the door.

Lillian stood beside him, her arms crossed, her expression thoughtful. "Rachel's hiding something," she said softly, not looking at him but at the door where Rachel had disappeared.

Nathan nodded, his jaw tightening. "She's running from someone," he said quietly. "I think he's close."

Lillian glanced at him, her brow furrowed with concern. "And what are you going to do?"

Nathan didn't answer right away. He had spent so long running from his own past that the thought of helping someone else face theirs felt strange—like he was stepping into unknown territory. But when he had looked into Rachel's eyes, he had seen something familiar. The same fear, the same desperation that had driven him to keep moving for so long.

"I'm going to help her," Nathan said finally, his voice steady. "I'm not letting her face this alone."

Lillian studied him for a moment, then nodded. "I hope you're right," she said softly. "For both your sakes."

Chapter Twenty-Five: Running Scared

The wind howled through the narrow streets of Millbrook, rattling windows and sending loose shutters clattering against the sides of the buildings. Nathan stood at the window of his small room at the Riverside Boarding House, staring out into the night, his mind heavy with the events of the day. He should have been sleeping—the exhaustion of repairing Thompson Supplies had settled deep into his bones—but sleep wouldn't come.

Not tonight. Rachel's words echoed in his head. "He's found me." The fear in her voice had been unmistakable, and it gnawed at him. He had seen that kind of fear before, in the eyes of men who had run from war, in the faces of people who had lost everything. It was the kind of fear that left a person hollow, always looking over their shoulder, waiting for the past to catch up to them.

But now, it wasn't just Rachel's fear that weighed on him. It was the knowledge that he had offered to help her—that he had stepped into her world of secrets, knowing full well that it could bring danger to them all. The knock at the door startled him. He turned, heart racing, half expecting Rachel to be standing there, but it wasn't her.

Lillian stood in the doorway, her coat pulled tightly around her, her face pale in the dim light. "Can I come in?" she asked softly.

Nathan nodded, stepping aside as she entered the room. "What's wrong?"

Lillian hesitated, glancing around the room as if trying to gather her thoughts. She wrung her hands together, something Nathan had rarely seen her do. Lillian was always composed, even when things were falling apart around her. But tonight, something was different.

"I'm worried," she admitted, her voice barely above a whisper. "About Rachel. About you."

Nathan frowned, closing the door behind her. "You don't need to worry about me."

"I can't help it," Lillian said, her eyes meeting his. "You've been helping everyone in this town, but who's helping you? Who's keeping you from falling apart?"

Nathan was silent for a moment, her words hitting deeper than he cared to admit. He had spent so long running, so long keeping his distance from everyone around him, that the thought of someone worrying about him felt foreign.

"I'm fine," he said finally, though the words felt hollow. Lillian stepped closer, her expression soft but serious. "You're not fine, Nathan. I see it. You're carrying so much… and now, with Rachel…"

Nathan shook his head, turning away from her. "I promised I'd help her," he said quietly. "She's running from something—someone—and I know what that's like. I can't just stand by and watch her suffer."

Lillian's voice softened. "And who's helping you with your suffering?"

Nathan didn't answer. He couldn't. The truth was, no one had helped him. Not since the day he had lost his family, not since the day he had decided that running was the only way to survive. But now, standing in this small room with Lillian, he felt the weight of it all crashing down on him—the guilt, the grief, the fear.

Before he could say anything, there was another knock at the door. This time, it was more urgent, louder. Nathan's heart skipped a beat as he opened the door to find Reverend James standing there, his face pale and anxious. "We've got trouble," the reverend said, his voice tight. "Rachel's gone."

Nathan, Lillian, and Reverend James rushed down the snow-covered streets toward the church. The cold stung their faces, but the sharp wind did little to slow them down. As they approached, they saw a small group gathered outside, lanterns casting flickering shadows on the snow. Earl, the blacksmith, stood near the entrance, his brow furrowed with concern. Mrs. Granger was beside him, clutching her shawl tightly as if trying to ward off the chill. Ryan, the young man who worked at the boarding house, was speaking with Mayor Thornton, his face pale with worry.

"She just vanished," Earl said, his voice gruff but tinged with fear. "No one's seen her since the meeting. And with that stranger lurking around…"

Nathan's stomach tightened. "We need to split up," he said, his voice steady despite the knot of anxiety building inside him. "She couldn't have gotten far in this weather."

Mayor Thornton nodded, his jaw set with determination. "We'll search every corner of this town. Someone check the fields; someone else take the riverbank."

"I'll check the old barn," Earl volunteered. "It's not far, and she might've tried to take shelter there."

"I'll go with you," Ryan offered. The boy's face was pale, but his voice was steady.

Nathan turned to Reverend James. "Take some of the others and check near the church and the cemetery." Reverend James nodded, his lantern swinging in his hand as he gathered a few of the townsfolk.

"I'll take Lillian and search the Willowbend River," Nathan said, glancing at her. "She might have gone there to think. It's quiet."

Nathan and Lillian made their way through the deepening snow, their lanterns lighting the path ahead. The wind whipped through the trees, howling like a distant cry. Every step felt heavy, the weight of the night pressing down on them.

"She was so scared," Lillian said softly, her voice barely carrying over the wind. "Do you think she… do you think she's in danger?"

Nathan's jaw tightened. "I don't know," he admitted. "But we have to find her before something happens."

They reached the banks of the Willowbend River, the narrow current still flowing despite the freezing temperatures. The moon cast an eerie glow over the water, reflecting off the snow-covered banks. Nathan stopped, scanning the area with his lantern. The river was quiet, the only sound the gentle rush of the water against the rocks.

But then, in the distance, near a cluster of trees, he saw something—a figure huddled near the water, barely visible in the faint light.

"Rachel!" Nathan called, his heart pounding as he and Lillian rushed toward the figure. When they reached her, they found Rachel sitting by the edge of the river, her arms wrapped tightly around her knees, her breath coming out in ragged gasps. Tears streaked her face, and her eyes were wide with fear.

"I can't… I can't do this," she whispered, her voice broken. "I thought I could keep running, but I can't. He'll find me. He always finds me."

Nathan knelt beside her, his breath coming out in heavy puffs as the cold air hit his lungs. "You don't have to run anymore," he said softly. "We'll protect you. You're not alone in this."

Rachel shook her head, her entire body trembling. "You don't understand. You don't know what he's capable of. I can't stay here. I can't put you all in danger."

Lillian knelt beside them, her voice gentle but filled with conviction. "Rachel, we're not going to let him hurt you. You're part of this town now, and we take care of our own."

Rachel looked up at them, her eyes filled with a mixture of fear and disbelief. "Why?" she whispered, her voice barely audible. "Why would you risk everything for me?" Nathan's voice was steady as he spoke.

"Because I know what it's like to lose everything. I know what it's like to think that running is the only way to survive. But it's not. You can stop running, Rachel. You can stay."

Rachel's breath came out in shallow, shaky gasps as she looked between Nathan and Lillian, her mind racing with the weight of their words. From behind them, Reverend James's lantern appeared through the trees. Earl, Ryan, and Mrs. Granger followed close behind, their faces etched with concern as they approached.

"Is she alright?" Reverend James asked softly, his eyes filled with worry.

Nathan glanced back at them, then returned his attention to Rachel. "She will be," he said quietly, his voice filled with a quiet determination. Rachel nodded slowly, though tears still streamed down her face.

"Okay," she whispered, her voice so soft it was almost lost in the wind.

The townsfolk gathered around her, their faces filled with relief. For a moment, they all stood in silence, the weight of the night still heavy on their hearts, but the feeling of unity strong.

As they helped Rachel to her feet and began the slow walk back to town, Nathan couldn't shake the feeling that the real battle was just beginning.

Chapter Twenty-Six: Freedom and Guilt

The morning sun filtered through the curtains, casting a soft glow over the Thompson Supply Store. It had been a quiet, uneventful day in Millbrook, with most of the townspeople going about their daily routines. Inside the store, Nathan and Lillian moved around, organizing shelves and assisting the few customers.

Rachel sat at the small table in the back of the store, her hands cradling a cup of tea. The scent of the warm drink filled the room, but Rachel's thoughts were far away. The fear that had gripped her for so long still gnawed at her, even in the safety of the quiet town. She had been running for so long—constantly looking over her shoulder and waiting for Harlan to find her.

As Nathan walked past her, he placed the morning newspaper on the table, not thinking much of it.

"I'll be outside if you need me," he said, offering her a small smile before stepping out.

Rachel absently reached for the paper, flipping it open to the front page. But as her eyes scanned the bold headlines, her breath caught in her throat.

There, in black and white, was the news she had never thought she'd see: Wanted Man Dies in Nashville Wreck.

Rachel's heart pounded as she read the details. Harlan Duval, her husband, had been killed in a one-vehicle car wreck near Nashville. The report said he had lost control of his car while taking a sharp curve, hitting a tree. The accident had happened late at night, and he had died instantly. Her hands began to tremble, the edges of the newspaper shaking as she stared at the words. It didn't seem real. For so long, she had lived in fear, constantly looking over her shoulder, waiting for Harlan to catch up to her. And now... he was gone.

The paper fell from her hands as she sank back into her chair, her mind spinning. She should have felt relief, but a strange sense of guilt washed over her. Relief was there, too—deep down—but it was buried beneath layers of conflicting emotions.

"I shouldn't be happy," she whispered to herself. "I shouldn't feel this way."

But the truth was, for the first time in years, she didn't have to run. She didn't have to hide. The man controlling her life for so long was no longer a threat. Her relief was undeniable, but a deep, unsettling guilt shadowed it. She bowed her head, her breath coming in short, uneven gasps as she tried to make sense of the flood of emotions surging through her.

The next day was Sunday, and the town gathered at Millbrook Church for their weekly service. The small church was filled with the soft murmur of voices as people took their seats, the sunlight streaming through the stained-glass windows, casting colorful patterns across the wooden pews. Rachel sat between Lillian and Nathan, her hands clasped tightly in her lap. Her mind was still reeling from the news about Harlan, and she hadn't yet shared it with anyone. She wasn't sure how to feel or how to talk about it. Part of her was still processing the idea that she no longer had to live in fear, but the guilt weighed heavy on her heart.

As the service began, Reverend James stepped to the pulpit, his voice gentle but powerful as he welcomed the congregation.

]"Today's service is about healing and finding peace," he began, eyes scanning the room. "Sometimes, we carry burdens for far too long. We hold onto fear, guilt, and pain, and it weighs us down. But the Lord tells us that we don't have to carry those burdens alone. We are called to release them into His hands, to find rest and peace in Him."

Rachel's breath caught in her throat as the reverend's words washed over her. She could feel the weight of her emotions pressing down on her, the guilt and relief warring inside her heart.

"The Lord is a God of second chances," Reverend James continued, his voice steady. "No matter what we've been through or what fear or pain we carry, we are never too far from His grace. He offers us healing, a chance to start anew."

Tears welled up in Rachel's eyes as she lowered her head. She had been carrying the weight of her fear for so long, the constant dread of Harlan finding her. And now, with him gone, she was left with the overwhelming guilt of feeling relieved. Was it wrong to feel that way? Was it wrong to want peace, even after everything she had endured?

Lillian glanced at Rachel, sensing her friend's inner turmoil. She reached out, gently placing a hand on Rachel's arm, offering silent support.

"You don't have to carry it alone," Lillian whispered.

Rachel swallowed hard, her tears threatening to spill over. She closed her eyes, praying silently for the strength to let go of the fear, the guilt, and the pain that had controlled her for so long.

As the reverend led the congregation in prayer, Rachel whispered her own prayer, asking for the peace that had always seemed so far away.

The following week, the town of Millbrook began its quiet preparations for Christmas. The air was cool but not bitter, and the skies were a clear, brilliant blue. A gentle chill that reminded the townspeople of the approaching holiday. For the first time in years, Rachel didn't feel the constant weight of fear pressing down on her. But the guilt lingered, a shadow that still haunted her thoughts. She had lived in fear of Harlan for so long that now, even with him gone, she didn't know how to feel free.

Nathan noticed the change in her. He saw the way she moved with a little less hesitation, a little less fear, but he also saw the weight she still carried.

"Rachel," Nathan said softly as they worked in the store together, "you don't have to feel guilty. You deserve to feel peace after everything you've been through."

Rachel looked up at him, her eyes filled with a mixture of relief and sorrow. "I know... but it's hard. I spent so long running. I never thought I'd be free of him." Nathan's voice was gentle but firm. "You are free. And it's okay to feel relieved."

Rachel managed a small smile, though her heart still ached with the weight of her conflicting emotions. "Thank you," she whispered, her voice barely audible. Nathan nodded, offering her a look of understanding. "You're not alone, Rachel. We're here with you."

Chapter Twenty-Seven: Embracing Peace

The sun shone brightly over Millbrook, its golden rays casting a soft, comforting light over the town. It was an unseasonably warm day for mid-December, with clear blue skies stretching endlessly overhead. The crispness of the air reminded everyone that Christmas was just around the corner, but the snow that often accompanied the season had yet to fall.

Inside the Thompson Supply Store, Rachel stood at the window, staring out at the quiet streets. Her thoughts drifted, swirling between the relief she felt over Harlan's death and the gnawing guilt that seemed to cling to her like a shadow.

She hadn't been able to stop thinking about the newspaper headline—Wanted Man Dies in Nashville Wreck—and the flood of emotions that had followed. It was strange to feel relieved and know that the man who had controlled her life for so long was gone. But with that relief came guilt, an overwhelming sense that she didn't deserve to feel at peace.

Harlan had been her husband, after all, and no matter what he had done, it felt wrong to be glad that he was dead. Rachel's hands tightened around the fabric of her dress, her breath coming out in slow, uneven puffs. The world outside seemed so peaceful, so quiet. But inside, her heart was a storm.

The soft sound of footsteps broke through her thoughts, and she turned to see Nathan approaching, his expression gentle. "Are you alright?" he asked, his voice quiet, concerned.

Rachel offered a small, strained smile. "I don't know," she admitted, her voice barely above a whisper. "I should feel… something more. But all I feel is relief. And guilt."

Nathan nodded, understanding flashing in his eyes. "It's okay to feel both. After everything you've been through, it's normal."

Rachel turned to the window, watching a group of children run down the street, their laughter carrying on the cool breeze. "I've spent so many years running. Hiding. And now, it's over. But it doesn't feel over."

Nathan stepped closer, his voice steady and comforting. "It's going to take time, Rachel. You've been living in fear for so long; letting go of that is hard. But you don't have to feel guilty for being relieved."

Rachel swallowed hard, her hands trembling slightly as she crossed her arms over her chest. "I just… I never imagined it would end this way."

Nathan's gaze softened. "None of us can control how things end. But we can choose what to do next."

Rachel looked up at him, her dark eyes filled with uncertainty. "What if I don't know what to do next?"

Nathan offered her a small, reassuring smile. "You don't have to figure it all out right now. Take it one day at a time. And you're not alone—you've got Lillian, me, and this whole town behind you."

A short while later, the store's front door opened, and Reverend James entered, his warm smile lighting up the room. After exchanging greetings with Nathan and Lillian, the reverend's gaze landed on Rachel seated in the back.

He walked over to her, his eyes filled with quiet understanding. "Mind if we take a walk, Rachel?" he asked softly.

Rachel hesitated, but something in the reverend's kind eyes made her feel safe. She nodded, rising from her seat as they stepped outside into the cool December air. They walked in silence for a while, the streets of Millbrook bathed in the soft light of late afternoon. The wind rustled gently through the bare trees, and the river's soft murmur filled the quiet spaces between them. Finally, they reached the small bench near the Willowbend River, and the reverend gestured for her to sit.

"I imagine you've been carrying a lot of heavy thoughts these past few days," Reverend James said gently, sitting beside her. His voice was calm and full of compassion.

Rachel stared down at her hands, her fingers twisting in her lap. "I don't know what to feel," she admitted. "I'm… relieved. But I feel guilty for feeling that way."

Reverend James nodded slowly, his expression understanding. "It's natural to feel conflicted, Rachel. After all, you've lived with fear and pain for so long. Now that Harlan is gone, your heart doesn't quite know how to handle the change."

Rachel's breath hitched, and she glanced up at him, her voice trembling. "But he was still my husband. How can I be relieved that he's… gone?"

The reverend's gaze softened. "Rachel, the pain you've been through is real. It's not wrong to feel relieved when a burden is lifted from you, even if it was tied to someone you once cared for. Sometimes, we carry guilt not because of what we've done, but because we feel we don't deserve peace."

Tears welled up in Rachel's eyes, her chest tightening as she spoke. "It's just… it's hard to let go of the fear. I've been running for so long, and now, I don't know how to stop."

Reverend James offered her a kind smile, reaching into his coat pocket and pulling out a small, well-worn Bible. "You're not alone in feeling that way. Many people, when faced with the end of a long struggle, don't know how to move forward. But I think this might help."

He opened the Bible and found the passage he had been thinking of, his voice steady as he began to read: "Cast all your anxiety on Him because He cares for you." —1 Peter 5:7

Rachel closed her eyes, the words washing over her like a wave of peace. For so long, she had carried her fear and guilt alone, but in this quiet moment by the river, she felt the first flicker of hope. Maybe, just maybe, she didn't have to carry it alone anymore.

Reverend James placed a gentle hand on her shoulder. "Rachel, it's okay to let go of the fear. It's okay to feel relieved. You don't have to carry this by yourself. God offers us peace—if we're willing to let Him take the weight from us."

Rachel nodded, tears slipping down her cheeks as she whispered, "Thank you, Reverend." He smiled warmly. "You're not alone in this journey. We're all here for you."

Later that evening, after Rachel had returned to the store, Lillian and Nathan sat by the fire in the small living space behind the store. The crackling of the flames filled the silence between them, the warmth of the fire creating a peaceful atmosphere.

Lillian glanced at Nathan, sensing the weight of his thoughts. "You've been quiet tonight," she said softly. "Is something on your mind?"

Nathan shifted in his seat, his jaw tightening slightly. "Just thinking about… everything. Harlan, Rachel, the past. I guess it's stirred up some old memories."

Lillian tilted her head, her eyes gentle. "Do you want to talk about it?"

Nathan hesitated, but the quiet comfort of the fire and Lillian's presence made him feel safe enough to open up. "I've been thinking about Leslie and Elizabeth," he admitted, his voice rough with emotion. "It's been years, but sometimes it feels like it just happened. Like the guilt never really left."

Lillian reached out, placing a comforting hand on his arm. "I'm so sorry, Nathan. I can't imagine what that's been like for you."

Nathan stared into the fire, his voice low. "I should have been there for Leslie after Elizabeth died. But I wasn't. I couldn't. And then… she was gone too."

Lillian sat quietly for a moment, her hand still resting on his arm. She could feel the weight of his guilt, the years of carrying that burden alone. Finally, she reached for the Bible on the table beside her, the same one she had turned to during her own times of struggle. "I want to read you something," she said softly, flipping through the pages until she found the passage she was looking for. She began to read, her voice steady and filled with warmth: "The Lord is close to the brokenhearted and saves those who are crushed in spirit." —Psalm 34:18

Nathan listened in silence, the words sinking deep into his heart. He had carried his pain for so long, but hearing Lillian's voice, hearing the words of Scripture, made him realize that he didn't have to carry it alone anymore.

Lillian looked up at him, her eyes filled with compassion. "We're not meant to carry our burdens alone, Nathan. Sometimes we have to let God in, let Him carry the weight that's too heavy for us."

Nathan swallowed hard, his throat tight with emotion. "I'm trying," he said quietly. Lillian smiled softly. "That's all He asks."

They sat together in silence, the warmth of the fire and the shared comfort of Scripture bringing a quiet peace to the room. In that moment, they both knew that healing would take time, but they were no longer alone in their struggles.

Nathan leaned back in his chair, the flickering light from the fire casting soft shadows across his face. His heart was still heavy with the memories of Leslie and Elizabeth, but Lillian's words had settled something deep inside him. The burden was still there, but it felt lighter—like he didn't have to carry it by himself anymore.

Lillian glanced at him, her face softening as she saw the shift in his posture. "We all carry something, Nathan," she said quietly. "But that doesn't mean we have to carry it forever. You're allowed to let go, even if it takes time."

Nathan nodded, his gaze still fixed on the flames. "I think I'm finally ready to try."

Lillian smiled, a small but genuine smile that reached her eyes. "Good," she said softly. "Because you deserve peace too."

They sat in the quiet of the evening, the fire crackling gently beside them, the weight of their shared stories lingering in the air. Outside, the wind rustled through the trees, but inside, it was calm. For the first time in a long while, both Nathan and Lillian felt a sense of quiet hope—hope that the future might hold something more than just memories of the past. The clock on the mantel chimed softly, signaling the late hour.

Nathan glanced at it, then back at Lillian. "It's getting late," he said, his voice low but peaceful. "We should probably turn in."

Lillian nodded, rising from her chair and stretching slightly. "Yes, it's been a long day."

"Thank you," he said softly. "For tonight. For listening."

Lillian's smile was warm and understanding. "We all need someone to listen, Nathan. And you've been that person for so many people. It's okay to let someone be that for you, too."

Nathan nodded, the weight of her words settling into his heart. He offered her a small smile before disappearing down the hallway.

Lillian stood for a moment in the quiet of the house, the warmth of the evening still lingering in the air. She glanced at the worn Bible on the table and gently closed it, feeling a sense of peace wash over her. The words she had shared with Nathan had helped her too, reminding her that even in the hardest moments, there was always hope.

As she turned off the lamp and made her way to her room, she whispered a quiet prayer—one for Nathan, for Rachel, for herself. And as the house settled into stillness, she felt a sense of calm, knowing that tomorrow would bring new possibilities, new beginnings, and a chance for healing—for all of them.

Chapter Twenty-Eight: A Christmas of Giving

The air was crisp but clear on Christmas morning in Millbrook. Though the snow had yet to fall, a soft chill lingered in the air, making the warmth of Millbrook Church all the more welcoming.

The church was adorned with modest garlands, wreaths, and a simple nativity scene at the front, reflecting the humble yet heartfelt spirit of the holiday. People from all over town began to arrive, gathering to celebrate the birth of Christ.

Inside the church, the warm glow of candles flickered along the walls, casting soft shadows across the congregation. Lillian, with Samuel and Grace beside her, stood near the back, greeting others as they arrived. She smiled as she watched the church slowly fill with friends and neighbors, their faces alight with the joy of the season.

Rachel, standing quietly by Lillian's side, took a deep breath. She felt a strange sense of peace here in Millbrook, though the fear of her past still lingered like a shadow. She hadn't revealed her real identity yet, but the desire for a new life—a life where she could leave the past behind—was strong.

Lillian had become her anchor in this small town, offering friendship, support, and understanding when Rachel needed it most.

"Look," Grace whispered excitedly, tugging on her mother's sleeve. "There's Jed, and he's brought his family!"

Lillian glanced up in surprise, her eyes widening as she saw Jed walking through the doors with his wife, Martha, and their three children. Jed had always been known for his reserved nature, keeping mostly to himself and hoarding supplies during the tough times.

But today, there was something different about him—something softer, more open. Jed's children—a girl and two boys—stood shyly beside their parents, their wide eyes taking in the sights of the church. Abigail, the eldest at twelve, had her father's serious expression, while Henry, ten, had a mischievous glint in his eye. Caleb, the youngest at eight, clung to his mother's side, his dark hair falling into his eyes.

Nathan, who was standing near the front, noticed Jed's arrival and made his way over. As Jed turned, their eyes met, and Nathan extended his hand, a warm smile on his face.

"Jed," Nathan said, shaking his hand firmly, "I'm glad you're here. It's good to see you."

Jed hesitated for a moment, but then returned the handshake, his grip strong. "I, uh… I brought some food," he said quietly, his voice gruff but sincere.

"Figured it was time to share what I've been holding onto. Times are tough for all of us."

Nathan's smile deepened, his appreciation evident. "You did the right thing, Jed. This means a lot, especially today."

Jed's gaze softened as he looked around the church, his eyes landing on his children, who were quietly taking their seats. "It was Martha who convinced me," he admitted with a small chuckle. "She reminded me that Christmas isn't about holding on to what we have—it's about giving."

Nathan nodded, his voice thoughtful. "She's right. It's a time to come together, to help one another."

Jed took a seat beside his family, his serious expression softened as he looked at the filled pews. It had been a long time since he felt this connected to the community. The burden of hoarding what little food they had now seemed foolish. Today, for the first time in years, he felt part of something bigger—something more meaningful than mere survival.

Meanwhile, Mrs. Granger had been busy in the kitchen, overseeing the preparation of the Christmas meal. Earl and Ryan had spent the previous day hunting, bringing back several rabbits and a young deer. The deer was a lucky catch for the winter season, and the rabbits, abundant in the nearby woods, added to the feast. The game had been carefully prepared, and Mrs. Granger, along with a few other women from the congregation, now worked to cook the meat and set up the tables for the Christmas meal. The smell of roasted venison and rabbit filled the air, mingling with the scent of fresh bread and roasted potatoes that others had contributed.

Though food was scarce, everyone had brought something—a few home-canned vegetables, small loaves of bread, jars of pickled beans. Together, they had created a meal that would feed the entire congregation, an act of true generosity during such hard times.

Lillian glanced at Mrs. Granger as she stirred a large pot over the open flame. "That smells wonderful," she remarked, smiling at the older woman. "We're lucky to have Earl and Ryan hunting for us."

Mrs. Granger chuckled, her hands deftly working as she basted the venison. "They were determined to bring something back for the Christmas meal. It's not much, but it'll do."

Lillian nodded, her heart warming at the sight of the town pulling together. Though times were tough, there was no shortage of generosity when it mattered most.

As the service began, the church quieted, and Reverend James took his place at the front of the room, his hands resting on the worn Bible that had guided him through many difficult times. He smiled warmly at the congregation, his voice filled with reverence as he began the Christmas sermon.

"For to us a child is born, to us a son is given, and the government will be on his shoulders. And he will be called Wonderful Counselor, Mighty God, Everlasting Father, Prince of Peace. Of the greatness of his government and peace there will be no end." —Isaiah 9:6-7

He paused, letting the words settle in the congregation's hearts before continuing. "These words, spoken centuries before the birth of Christ, remind us that even in times of uncertainty, the Prince of Peace is with us. Though we may face hardships, as we have in this past year, the promise of peace is ever-present."

Reverend James closed the Bible, but his voice grew stronger as he spoke from the heart. "We've all been through difficult times. We've seen loss, we've experienced fear, and many of us have struggled to find hope. But today, we gather not just to celebrate the birth of our Savior, but to celebrate the hope that He brings."

As he spoke, the congregation listened intently, their hearts touched by his words. Samuel and Grace beside Lillian, their wide eyes fixed on the reverend.

Grace whispered excitedly to her brother, "Do you think the angels were really there when Jesus was born?"

Samuel smiled, his serious expression softening. "Yeah. I think they were. And maybe they're still watching over us."

Lillian placed a hand on each of their shoulders, smiling at their innocent wonder. The simplicity of their faith was a reminder of the purity of Christmas—a reminder that even in the darkest times, there was always light.

Reverend James continued, his voice growing more passionate as he spoke of Christ's birth. "Mary and Joseph had very little that night in Bethlehem, but they had something far more valuable—the promise of God's love, the hope of salvation for all. And today, we celebrate that same love and hope. No matter what we face, we know that God is with us."

As the reverend spoke, Rachel felt a lump rise in her throat. She had spent so long running, hiding, and fearing the world. But here, in this small church, surrounded by people who cared for her even without knowing her true identity, she felt something she hadn't felt in years—peace.

She glanced over at Lillian, who smiled warmly at her, and Rachel knew that she was no longer alone. Reverend James paused for a moment, looking out over the congregation, his voice softening as he prepared to close the service.

"Let us remember the words of the angels on that holy night: 'Glory to God in the highest, and on earth peace, goodwill toward men.' May we carry that peace and goodwill with us today, and always."

As the service came to a close, the congregation joined together in song, their voices filling the church with the sweet melody of "Silent Night."

The sound was pure, unadorned, but it resonated with a depth of emotion that left many with tears in their eyes.

After the service, the congregation gathered for the meal, everyone pitching in to help. Nathan made his way over to Jed again, this time offering him a plate of food as a gesture of gratitude. The two men stood side by side, watching their families and friends share in the meal, their hearts lighter for having come together on this special day. Rachel and Lillian shared a quiet moment, standing near the fire as the rest of the congregation enjoyed the meal.

"Thank you," Rachel said softly, her voice filled with emotion. "For everything." Lillian smiled, her eyes warm.

"You don't have to thank me. You've become family here, Rachel. You're one of us."

Rachel blinked back tears, her heart full. "I'm starting to believe that."

Chapter Twenty-Nine: Signs of Change

The rain began to fall softly, a steady patter against the roof of Mrs. Granger's home as Rachel sat quietly by the fireplace. She listened to the rhythmic tapping of the droplets against the window, each a reminder of the growing storm outside. A chill hung in the air, not from the cold but from anticipating what was coming.

Across from her sat Ryan, his dark eyes reflecting the flickering flames of the fire. His usual quiet demeanor seemed heavier tonight, as though the storm outside was echoing the storm within him. The silences between them had been comfortable before, but something lingered in the space tonight—an unspoken tension.

"I've been thinking," Ryan finally said, his voice low but clear. His eyes flickered toward Rachel, studying her reaction. "About staying here in Millbrook. I've been moving from place to place for so long, and it feels like I belong somewhere for the first time."

Rachel nodded slowly, unsure of what to say. She understood that feeling more than anyone—running, trying to find a place to call home. But could Millbrook really be that place for her? Could she ever stop running?

Ryan shifted in his seat, leaning forward slightly, his elbows resting on his knees. "And," he added, his voice soft but steady, "I like spending time with you, Rachel."

Rachel's heart skipped a beat, her eyes flicking to meet his. There it was—the weight of what had been lingering between them. She had sensed it, the way he looked at her, the kindness he showed, but she hadn't been ready to acknowledge it. Not yet. Maybe not ever.

"I…" Rachel started, her voice catching in her throat. She wasn't sure how to respond. She had grown fond of Ryan. That much was true. He had been kind to her, and maybe things would be different in a different life. But her past—her fear—was too much to overcome.

"I like spending time with you too," she finally said, her voice soft, almost apologetic. "But I don't know if I'm ready for… anything more. Not right now."

Ryan's gaze softened, and though there was a flicker of disappointment in his eyes, he nodded. "I understand," he said gently, offering her a small, sad smile. "I just… wanted you to know. I'm not trying to push you, Rachel. I just thought… maybe, in time."

Rachel swallowed hard, her hands twisting nervously in her lap. "I don't know if time will change anything," she admitted quietly. "I've been through a lot… and I'm still figuring out how to move forward."

Ryan nodded again, understanding flashing in his eyes. "Take all the time you need," he said softly. "I'll be here. As a friend, if nothing else."

Rachel's heart ached at his words, at the sincerity in his voice. She wanted to say something more that would ease the tension between them, but the words wouldn't come. Instead, she offered him a small, grateful smile, hoping it would be enough for now.

Outside, the storm was intensifying. The wind howled through the trees, and the distant rumble of thunder echoed across the dark sky. Nathan stood outside Reverend James' home, pulling his coat tighter around him as he knocked on the door. The storm had brought with it an unease he couldn't quite shake, a restlessness that seemed to mirror the uncertainty in his own heart. The door creaked open, and Reverend James greeted him warmly.

"Come in, Nathan. It's getting wild out there." Nathan stepped inside, the warmth of the reverend's home enveloping him as he shook off the cold. The smell of tea and burning wood filled the air, a comforting contrast to the storm raging outside.

Reverend James motioned for him to sit by the fire, where two steaming cups of tea awaited. "I've been wanting to talk to you," the reverend said as he sat across from Nathan. His eyes were kind but probing, as though he could see the weight Nathan carried with him, the burden he'd been holding for far too long.

Nathan shifted uncomfortably, sensing where this conversation was heading. "I'm fine, Reverend," he said gruffly, not meeting the older man's gaze. "Just doing my part, trying to get by."

Reverend James smiled knowingly, leaning forward slightly. "We both know there's more to it than that, Nathan. You've been doing more than just getting by. You've been helping this town, helping others, but when's the last time you let someone help you?"

Nathan stiffened, his jaw tightening. He didn't like being called out, especially not when it came to matters of the heart or faith. "I don't need help," he muttered, his voice rough. "I've been fine on my own."

The reverend nodded slowly as though considering his words carefully. "I understand," he said after a long pause. "But sometimes, Nathan, getting by isn't enough. We're not meant to carry everything on our own. That's why I wanted to give you something."

Reverend James reached into his coat pocket and pulled out a small, well-worn Bible. Its pages were yellowed, and the cover was creased from years of use. He placed it gently on the table between them, his eyes never leaving Nathan's.

"I want you to have this," the reverend said softly. "It's helped me through many hard times, and I think it could help you too."

Nathan stared at the Bible, his chest tightening. Not since everything had fallen apart. He hadn't picked up a Bible in years. He wasn't sure he could accept it—wasn't sure if he even deserved it.

"I don't know," Nathan muttered, shaking his head. "I'm not the kind of man who…"

"Who what?" Reverend James interrupted gently. "Who's perfect? None of us are, Nathan. That's not what this is about. It's about finding peace. It's about letting go of the burdens you've been carrying for so long."

Nathan swallowed hard, his throat tight. Slowly, he reached out and took the Bible, his hands trembling slightly as he ran his fingers over the worn cover. "I'll think about it," he said quietly.

Reverend James smiled, his eyes filled with understanding. "That's all I ask."

Later that evening, as the storm continued to rage outside, Rachel found herself at Lillian's home. The warmth of the fire crackled in the hearth, and the smell of fresh bread filled the air. Samuel and Grace played quietly on the floor, their laughter a sweet contrast to the thunder rumbling outside.

Lillian sat beside Rachel, offering her a cup of tea. "It's good to see you," she said softly. "The kids have been asking about you."

Rachel smiled, her heart warming at the thought of Samuel and Grace. They had become like family to her, a source of comfort in a world that still felt uncertain.

"I've missed them," she admitted, her eyes softening as she watched them play.

"They adore you," Lillian said with a smile. "You've brought so much joy to their lives, Rachel. You've become family here."

Rachel's chest tightened with emotion. Family. It was a word she hadn't allowed herself to think about in a long time. She had been running for so long, hiding from the life she had left behind, that she had forgotten what it felt like to belong somewhere.

"I don't know what I'd do without you, Lillian," Rachel whispered, her voice thick with emotion. "You've given me a place to feel safe."

Lillian reached out and placed a hand on Rachel's arm, her eyes warm with understanding. "You don't have to thank me," she said softly. "We're all in this together."

As the year drew to a close, the storm began to subside, leaving the town in a quiet calm. The sound of raindrops tapping gently against the roof was the only noise left from the passing storm.

Inside, the warmth of the fire and the companionship of friends brought a sense of peace—a peace that had been hard-won but was cherished all the more because of it.

The town of Millbrook was preparing for a new year with all the uncertainty and hope it would bring. As the clock ticked closer to 1934, Rachel, Nathan, and the others knew they weren't alone in facing whatever the future held. They had each other, and in this small town, that was enough.

Chapter Thirty: The Unburdening

The first light of dawn crept through the clouds, casting a pale glow over Millbrook as Nathan worked alone by the church. His hands moved methodically, mending the weathered fence that had stood for years, but his mind was elsewhere—lost in the memories that had resurfaced after the Christmas service. The peace he had felt briefly seemed to slip through his fingers, replaced by the familiar weight of guilt and regret.

His thoughts drifted back to Leslie and Elizabeth. He could still see their faces, still hear their laughter, but it was always followed by the pain—the memory of losing them, the suffocating feeling of failure. He had tried so hard to bury it, to move on, but the past clung to him like a shadow. As he worked, the sound of footsteps approached. He didn't need to turn to know it was Lillian. She had a way of finding him when he needed someone most, even when he didn't want to admit it.

"You've been out here for hours," Lillian said gently, standing by the fence. "Why don't you come inside and rest for a while?"

Nathan didn't respond at first, his grip tightening on the hammer in his hand. He wasn't sure he wanted to talk, but something in him, something tired and worn, was beginning to unravel.

"I can't rest," he muttered, his voice rough. "Not with all this in my head."

Lillian stepped closer, her eyes filled with understanding. "You don't have to carry it alone, Nathan. You never did."

For a long moment, Nathan was silent. The fence in front of him blurred as his thoughts raced. He had been carrying this burden for so long that he wasn't sure he could put it down or even knew how. But as he stood there, the familiar ache in his chest tightening, he realized he couldn't do it anymore. He couldn't keep pretending.

"It was my fault," Nathan said quietly, his voice barely a whisper. "What happened to Leslie, to Elizabeth... I should have been there for them. I should have protected them."

Lillian's heart ached at the pain in his voice. She had known that Nathan carried guilt, but hearing it laid bare like this was more than she had expected. She stepped closer, placing a hand gently on his arm.

"You did everything you could, Nathan," she said softly. "Sometimes, no matter how hard we try, things happen that are beyond our control."

Nathan shook his head, his voice breaking. "I wasn't there for them when they needed me most. I failed them."

Tears welled in Lillian's eyes, but she held them back, knowing Nathan needed her strength.

"You didn't fail them, Nathan. You loved them. And sometimes, love means letting go of our guilt, even when it feels impossible."

Nathan's shoulders slumped, and he let the tears come for the first time in years. He had been holding it all inside for so long, trying to be strong, but its weight had finally become too much. "I don't know how to let it go," he whispered, his voice hoarse.

Lillian stood beside him, offering the comfort of her presence. "You don't have to do it alone," she said gently. "I've been where you are, Nathan. I've carried my own burdens, my own regrets."

Nathan turned to her, surprised. "You?"

Lillian nodded, her gaze distant as she remembered. "When my husband died, I blamed myself for a long time. If I had done things differently and been stronger, maybe he'd still be here. But over time, I realized that holding on to that guilt wasn't helping anyone. It wasn't bringing him back, and it wasn't helping my children. I had to learn to forgive myself."

Nathan stared at her, his mind swirling with emotions. He had never thought of Lillian as someone who carried the same kind of pain he did. But hearing her speak, seeing the strength in her despite what she had been through, gave him a glimmer of hope.

"I don't know if I can do that," he said quietly. "Forgive myself."

Lillian smiled softly, her hand still resting on his arm. "It's not easy. But it's possible. And I'll be here every step of the way."

Meanwhile, Rachel stood by the river, the wind tugging at her coat as she stared at the water. The weight of the past weeks hung heavy on her, the newspaper article still fresh in her mind. Everyone in town knew her last name was Duval, but they hadn't pushed her or asked questions about who she really was.

But Rachel knew it was only a matter of time before the truth came out—before they realized who she really was, what she had been running from. The thought of it made her heart race. She had found something here in Millbrook—a sense of peace, of belonging—but it was built on a lie. Could she ever truly start over if she was still hiding from the truth?

She turned, startled, as Ryan approached from the path behind her. His usual easy smile was gone, replaced by a look of concern.

"You've been quiet lately," he said, coming to stand beside her. "Is everything all right?"

Rachel forced a small smile, though it didn't reach her eyes. "I'm fine," she said, her voice strained. Ryan wasn't convinced. He had grown fond of Rachel, and he could see the weight she was carrying.

"You don't have to pretend with me, Rachel. I can tell something's bothering you."

Rachel's heart pounded as she met his gaze. She had been avoiding this conversation, avoiding the moment when she would have to tell him the truth. But how could she? How could she tell him about the woman she had been, the life she had left behind?

"I…" She hesitated, her voice trembling. "It's complicated, Ryan."

Ryan stepped closer, his eyes softening. "I know things have been hard for you, and I don't want to push you. But whatever you carry, you don't have to carry it alone."

Rachel swallowed hard, the lump growing as the words she held back threatened to spill over. "It's just… I've made mistakes. I've been running for so long and don't know how to stop."

Ryan looked at her for a long moment, his expression filled with compassion.

"Rachel, we all have things we're running from. But this town… these people… they don't care about your past. They care about who you are now."

Tears welled in Rachel's eyes, and she quickly wiped them away. "What if they don't understand?"

Ryan's voice was gentle. "I think you'll be surprised. People here… they know about second chances."

Back at the house, Lillian sat with Nathan, both feeling the weight of the conversation they'd just had. The room was quiet, save for the soft crackle of the fire.

Nathan glanced at the Bible Reverend James had given him earlier. It sat on the table between them, untouched. "I haven't opened it," Nathan admitted, his voice low.

Lillian smiled gently. "It's okay. When you're ready, you will."

Nathan looked down at his hands, his mind still racing. "Do you really think there's a way to let go of all this?"

Lillian met his gaze. Her voice was soft but firm. "I do. And I think it starts with believing that you deserve it."

Chapter Thirty-One: Spirituality

The soft patter of rain against the window created a steady rhythm in Mrs. Granger's home. The fireplace crackled quietly, casting a warm glow over the small room. Ryan and Rachel sat together on the worn sofa, their knees almost touching, but the space between them felt charged with unspoken words.

Rachel stared into the flames, her heart heavy with the weight of her past. She had kept so much hidden, even after everything that had happened, and though she trusted Ryan more than most, it was still hard to let herself be vulnerable. Sensing her hesitance, Ryan leaned forward, resting his elbows on his knees. His dark eyes reflected the flickering firelight, but his voice was soft when he spoke.

"You don't have to tell me anything, Rachel," he said gently. "I just want you to know I'm here if you ever feel like talking."

Rachel looked at him, her chest tightening. Something about Ryan—his quiet strength and unwavering patience— made her feel safe in a way she hadn't felt in years.

She swallowed hard, knowing it was time to let him in, at least a little.

"I've been running for a long time," she admitted quietly, her gaze drifting back to the fire. "From everything—my past, my mistakes, my… my husband." Her voice wavered slightly on the last word, and she saw Ryan's expression harden, though he didn't say anything. Ryan remained still, giving her the space to continue. "I thought if I kept moving, maybe he wouldn't find me. Maybe I could disappear. But even here, in Millbrook... it's hard to let go of that fear."

Ryan's voice was calm, but there was a quiet intensity behind it. "You don't have to keep running anymore, Rachel. This town... these people... they care about you. You've built something here. You're not alone."

Rachel bit her lip, her heart pounding in her chest. "I know. I know I'm not alone anymore, but it's hard to believe everything won't disappear again. Whenever I feel like I've found peace, something reminds me of who I used to be."

Ryan shifted closer, his hand resting gently on her arm. "You're not the same person you were, Rachel. We all have things we're ashamed of. I've done things I'm not proud of, too."

Rachel looked at him, surprised. "You?"

Ryan nodded, his eyes softening. "Before I came here, I spent a lot of time doing things I'm not proud of. I was angry, lost... but this town gave me a second chance. And you deserve one, too."

Tears welled in Rachel's eyes, and she quickly wiped them away. "Thank you, Ryan. I don't know if I'll ever stop being afraid, but... it feels better not to face it alone."

Ryan smiled, his hand still resting on her arm. "You don't have to face anything alone anymore, Rachel."

At the boarding house, the storm outside seemed to echo Nathan's inner turmoil. He sat at the small desk in his room. The Bible Reverend James had given him lying unopened in front of him. For years, he had distanced himself from faith, from the God he had once believed in. But something had shifted after the Christmas service, something deep and unnamable.

His fingers hovered over the worn cover, the weight of his past pressing down on him as he hesitated. He had never been the kind of man to cry easily, even after losing Elizabeth and Leslie. The grief had been too big, too consuming for tears. But now, as he sat alone in the quiet of the room, the memories came rushing back.

Slowly, he opened the Bible, the pages crackling softly under his touch. He wasn't sure where to start, but as he thumbed through the thin pages, his eyes fell on a passage from Isaiah: "Do not fear, for I am with you; do not be dismayed, for I am your God. I will strengthen you and help you; I will uphold you with my righteous right hand." —Isaiah 41:10

The words seemed to leap off the page, piercing through the walls he had built around his heart. He stared at them for a long moment, his chest tightening. Tears pricked at his eyes, but he blinked them back, shaking his head.

"No," he whispered to himself. "Not yet."

But as the silence of the room closed in around him, he found himself turning the pages again, his eyes scanning until they landed on another verse from Matthew: "Come to me, all you who are weary and burdened, and I will give you rest." —Matthew 11:28

The words hit him like a blow to the chest. Weary. Burdened. He had been carrying his guilt for so long, too long. And in that moment, something inside him broke. The first tear slipped down his cheek, and then another. Before he knew it, the dam had broken, and he was crying—really crying—for the first time since he had lost his family.

The sobs wracked his body, and he buried his face in his hands, the Bible still open in front of him. For so long, he had believed that he didn't deserve forgiveness, that he didn't deserve peace. But now, as the tears flowed freely, he felt something else—something warm, something that felt like hope. He wasn't sure how long he sat there, his shoulders shaking as the storm raged outside.

But when the tears finally subsided, he felt lighter, as if some of the weight he had been carrying had been lifted. The words of the Bible still echoed in his mind, offering him a sliver of peace he hadn't felt in years.

Meanwhile, in the quiet warmth of her home, Lillian sat with Samuel and Grace. The fire crackled softly in the hearth, and the storm outside seemed distant, almost peaceful. The children sat beside her, their eyes wide with curiosity as they sensed that their mother had something important to say. Lillian took a deep breath, her hands resting in her lap. She had been carrying the memory of their father in her heart for so long, unsure of how to share it with them. But now, as they grew older, she knew it was time.

"There's something I've been meaning to talk to you about," she began softly, her voice steady despite the swirl of emotions inside her. "It's about your father."

Samuel and Grace exchanged glances, their expressions filled with curiosity. "You've told us some things before," Samuel said quietly, his tone mature for his age. "But not much."

Lillian nodded, a small smile tugging at the corners of her mouth. "I know. And that's because… it was hard for me to talk about him. But I think it's time you knew more." She paused, gathering her thoughts before continuing. "Your father was a good man. He loved you both very much. But… life was hard for him. He struggled with things I couldn't always help him with. And when he passed, I… I had to be strong for you."

Grace's eyes shimmered with unshed tears, and Samuel's face grew serious. "How did he die?" Grace asked, her voice small.

Lillian swallowed hard, her heart aching as she met her daughter's gaze. "He got very sick, Grace. It wasn't his fault. He tried so hard to get better, but… sometimes, things happen that we can't control."

Samuel reached out and took his mother's hand, his small fingers squeezing hers. "We miss him," he said quietly.

Lillian's eyes filled with tears, but were not the heavy tears of grief. They were tears of release, of finally sharing the burden she had carried for so long. "I miss him too," she whispered. "Every day."

The three of them sat in silence for a while, the warmth of the fire wrapping around them like a comforting embrace. And for the first time, Lillian felt a sense of peace, knowing that her children finally understood a part of their past that had been too painful to share before.

Chapter Thirty-Two: New Beginnings in Millbrook

The first light snow of January drifted gently from the sky, blanketing the small town of Millbrook in a soft white glow. The air was crisp but not harsh, and the townspeople made their way to the church, their boots crunching softly against the fresh snow. There was a quiet stillness in the air, a sense of peace that had settled over the town as they gathered for the first Sunday service of the new year. Inside the church, the warmth of the fire in the hearth and the soft glow of candles filled the room with a welcoming light.

Reverend James stood at the front, his Bible resting in his hands as the congregation began to fill the pews, their breaths still visible in the cold air. Nathan entered quietly, his steps slow and thoughtful. He glanced around, taking in the sight of familiar faces, the people who had become more than just neighbors—they had become family.

His gaze lingered on Lillian, who sat with Samuel and Grace, their eyes bright with excitement. The children waved at him, and he offered them a small smile before taking his seat near the front. Beside him, Rachel sat quietly, her heart still heavy with the weight of her past but lighter than it had been in years. She glanced at Ryan, who smiled warmly at her, and for the first time, she felt a small sense of hope—a sense that maybe, just maybe, she could finally stop running.

In the pews just behind them, Jed sat with his wife, Martha, and their three children, Abigail, Henry, and Caleb. The change in Jed over the past few weeks had been remarkable. He no longer hoarded supplies or kept them to himself, and today, he even offered to help clear the snow from the church steps before the service. It was a small gesture that spoke volumes about the man he was becoming.

As the last of the congregation took their seats, Reverend James stood before them, his voice filled with warmth and reverence as he opened the service.

"Good morning," he began, his eyes scanning the room filled with familiar faces. "It is a blessing to gather here today to start this new year together, united in faith and community." He paused, his voice softening as he continued. "We've been through so much this past year. We've faced hardships, lost loved ones, and struggled to make it through. But through it all, we've found strength in each other and in the love of God."

Reverend James opened his Bible, his fingers resting on the pages as he read from Psalm 46: "God is our refuge and strength, an ever-present help in trouble. Therefore we will not fear, though the earth give way and the mountains fall into the heart of the sea, though its waters roar and foam and the mountains quake with their surging." —Psalm 46:1-3

The words filled the church, echoing in the hearts of the congregation. Nathan felt the familiar weight of his past lifting if only a little. The promise of strength and refuge spoke to something deep inside him—a reminder that there was always a way back no matter how far he had fallen.

Reverend James looked up from the Bible, his eyes resting on the faces of the people he had come to love. "These words remind us that we are never alone. Even in the darkest moments, even when the world seems to be crumbling around us, we have a refuge. God is with us."

He closed the Bible gently, but his voice grew stronger as he continued. "In this past year, we have seen struggles. We've faced hard times together. But we've also seen something else—something more powerful. We've seen what it means to love and support each other through those difficult times. And we've seen the strength that comes not from ourselves but God."

His gaze swept across the room, resting on each for a moment.

"It doesn't matter where we've come from, what we've done, or how many times we've fallen. God's grace is greater than all of it. And when we lean on Him and each other, there is nothing we can't overcome."

The congregation sat in quiet reflection, the light snow tapping gently against the windows, creating a peaceful backdrop to the reverend's words. Rachel closed her eyes, taking a deep breath as the message settled in her heart. She wasn't sure what the future held for her, but for the first time, she felt she had found a place where she could belong.

Reverend James opened his Bible again, his voice steady as he read from Jeremiah 29: "For I know the plans I have for you," declares the Lord, "plans to prosper you and not to harm you, plans to give you hope and a future." —Jeremiah 29:11

The words hung in the air, filled with promise and hope. Nathan felt something stir deep inside him—a warmth that he hadn't felt in years. He wasn't sure what the future held for him, but for the first time, he wasn't afraid to face it. He had found peace and maybe even a sense of redemption.

As the service concluded, the congregation slowly made their way out of the church, their breath visible in the cold January air. The snow had stopped falling, leaving a soft blanket of white across the town.

The streets of Millbrook looked serene, untouched, and peaceful—a fitting backdrop for the new beginning that so many in the town felt. Nathan stood just outside the church, looking out over the town as the people dispersed, heading home or toward the Thompson Supply Store, where Lillian had invited some of the townsfolk to gather for a light meal.

Nathan lingered for a moment, breathing in the cold air, his thoughts quieter than they had been in years. He noticed Jed standing by his wagon, helping his wife and children settle in for the ride home. Nathan had always thought of Jed as a distant man, but something about him had changed. There was a lightness in the way he spoke to his children, a gentleness that hadn't been there before.

Nathan approached, his boots crunching in the snow as he walked over. "Jed," he said, offering him a smile. "That was a nice service."

Jed turned, his face thoughtful, and nodded. "Yeah, it was. Makes you think about things... about how far we've come." He paused, glancing at his family, then back at Nathan. "I've been thinking a lot lately. About what I've been holding onto and needing to let go of."

Nathan understood the weight of those words better than most. "It's not easy," he said quietly. "But it's worth it." Jed gave a short nod, his eyes filled with something deeper, something close to gratitude. "Yeah. It is." As Jed climbed into the wagon with his family, Nathan watched them drive away, a smile tugging at the corners of his mouth. Jed was changing, just like he was. And it was good to see.

Later that afternoon, many townspeople gathered at the Thompson Supply Store, the smell of warm bread and hot coffee filling the air. Mrs. Granger and Lillian had worked together to prepare a small meal for everyone—a simple gathering, but one that felt right for the close-knit community they had become.

Nathan stood behind the counter, helping Ryan unload supplies while the others sat around the tables, sharing quiet conversations and warm smiles. The store had become more than just a place to buy supplies—where the townspeople gathered, shared their burdens, and found comfort in each other. Rachel stood near the back, talking quietly with Lillian. The two women had grown close over the past weeks, their bond deepening as Rachel had begun to open up more about her past. Their conversation was lighter today—filled with warmth and laughter.

"I never thought I'd feel at home in a place like this," Rachel admitted, glancing around the store. Lillian smiled, her eyes soft. "You've found your place here, Rachel. And we're all better for having you."

Rachel looked at Lillian, her heart full. "Thank you," she whispered. "For everything."

As the evening drew to a close, Nathan found himself walking down the familiar path toward the Willowbend River, the snow crunching beneath his boots. The air was still, the sky a soft shade of pink as the sun set in the distance. It had become a habit of his to visit the river when he needed time to think, and today was no different.

The Bible Reverend James had given him was tucked inside his coat, and for a moment, Nathan considered taking it out, reading another passage. But today, he didn't need the words to find peace. He had found it in the people around him, in the quiet strength of the town, and in the hope that the new year had brought.

As he stood there, he heard the soft crunch of footsteps behind him. Turning, he saw Lillian approaching, her auburn hair catching the last rays of the setting sun. "You come here a lot," she said with a smile, her breath visible in the cold air.

Nathan nodded, his eyes returning to the river. "It's quiet here. Helps me think."

Lillian stood beside him, the silence between them comfortable. After a moment, she spoke softly. "I've been thinking a lot lately, too. About the future. About the past."

Nathan glanced at her, his brow furrowed. "You don't have to carry it all on your own, Lillian. You've been a rock for everyone else. It's okay to let someone be there for you."

Lillian smiled, her eyes softening as she looked at him. "I know. And I think I'm ready for that."

Nathan reached out, gently taking her hand in his. "We'll face it together."

They stood by the river for a while longer, the sounds of the town behind them growing faint as the sun dipped lower in the sky.

It was peaceful here—just the two of them, surrounded by the quiet strength of nature and the warmth of their growing connection. At that moment, Nathan knew that whatever the future held, he wouldn't have to face it alone.

Back in the town square, the last few families were making their way home as the stars began to appear in the darkening sky. Reverend James stood by the church, watching the townspeople go about their lives with a quiet sense of satisfaction. Millbrook had faced its share of hardships, but they had come through it stronger than ever.

Rachel and Ryan walked side by side, their voices low but filled with the quiet joy of new beginnings. Ryan glanced at Rachel, his eyes warm and full of admiration.

"You're stronger than you think," he said gently.

Rachel looked up at him, her dark eyes reflecting the starlight. "Maybe," she whispered. "But I'm not ready for more."

Ryan nodded. His voice was soft but understanding. "I'm not going anywhere. Whenever you're ready, I'll be here."

Rachel felt a warmth spread through her chest. She wasn't sure if she'd ever be ready, but the knowledge that she had found a place to start over and be herself was enough for now.

As the snow continued to fall softly, Jed and his family walked down the main street, the sound of their children's laughter filling the air. He exchanged a glance with Martha, and for the first time in years, Jed felt at peace. He had let go of the fear that had kept him isolated for so long. Now, with his family by his side, he felt like he had finally come home.

In the quiet stillness of the town, Reverend James' final words from the morning service echoed in everyone's hearts: "God is our refuge and strength."

For the people of Millbrook, those words had never felt truer. As they faced the new year, they did so with the knowledge that they were stronger, united in faith and love. The light snow that fell from the sky was not a sign of winter's chill but a reminder of the purity and grace they had all found.

The past year's trials brought them closer—to each other and God. As they stepped into the future, they did so with the quiet confidence that they would never walk alone.

Made in the USA
Columbia, SC
25 March 2025